His voice seemed to hold a distinct note of...anger.

Anger. The small elusive thread of recognition that had tugged at her memory before it suddenly became a thick cord of garroting strength, whipping tightly around her, paralyzing her vocal cords, making her shake with shock, the cold sweat of fear springing from her pores.

No. It was impossible. It just couldn't be. She was imagining things. That voice, Gideon's voice was not....

She was still clutching the receiver, even though the line had gone dead. She was completely alone in the empty room, only the echo of Gideon's voice to remind her.... Just as, all those years ago, she had also only been left with the echo of a bitterly angry and contemptuous male voice....

PENNY JORDAN was constantly in trouble in school because of her inability to stop daydreaming—especially during French lessons. In her teens, she was an avid romance reader, although it didn't occur to her to try writing one herself until she was older. "My first half-dozen attempts ended up ingloriously," she remembers, "but I persevered, and one manuscript was finished." She plucked up the courage to send it to a publisher, convinced her book would be rejected. It wasn't, and the rest is history! Penny is married and lives in Cheshire.

Penny Jordan's striking mainstream novel *Power Play* quickly became a *New York Times* bestseller. She followed that success with *Silver*, *The Hidden Years*, *Lingering Shadows*, *For Better For Worse* and *Cruel Legacy*.

"Women everywhere will find pieces of themselves in Jordan's characters."
　　　—*Publishers Weekly* on *For Better For Worse*

Don't miss Penny's latest blockbuster, *Power Games*, available mid-1996.

Books by Penny Jordan

HARLEQUIN PRESENTS
1673—LESSON TO LEARN
1705—LAW OF ATTRACTION
1719—A MATTER OF TRUST
1734—TUG OF LOVE
1746—PASSIONATE POSSESSION
1756—PAST LOVING
1774—YESTERDAY'S ECHOES

PENNY JORDAN

An Unforgettable Man

Harlequin Books

TORONTO • NEW YORK • LONDON
AMSTERDAM • PARIS • SYDNEY • HAMBURG
STOCKHOLM • ATHENS • TOKYO • MILAN
MADRID • WARSAW • BUDAPEST • AUCKLAND

ISBN 0-373-11805-8

AN UNFORGETTABLE MAN

First North American Publication 1996.

This edition published by arrangement with Harlequin Books S.A.

® and TM are trademarks of the publisher. Trademarks indicated with ® are registered in the United States Patent and Trademark Office, the Canadian Trade Marks Office and in other countries.

Printed in U.S.A.

CHAPTER ONE

COURAGE just managed to stop herself making the betrayingly nervous gesture of smoothing down the skirt of her suit—a copy of a Chanel design she had had made up in Hong Kong for a tenth of the cost of the original—not that there was anyone else in the room to witness any potential breach in her composure. She was, it seemed, the final candidate to be interviewed for the post of household comptroller to the millionaire businessman Gideon Reynolds.

In normal circumstances she would not have been anything like this nervous; she had faced far stiffer interviews than this one in her career. But she had never wanted a job—any job—as desperately as she did this one. And it made no difference reminding herself that she was qualified for it—too well-qualified in many ways. The talents and training of an award-winning management executive of a chain of prestige European conference-centre hotels did not transfer very well to the job opportunities of a sleepy Dorset market town.

She had spent the last week working part-time stacking the shelves at a local supermarket and very glad of the money she had earned there she had been, as well.

The trouble was that the hotel trade, even at her relatively high level, did not pay particularly well. In the past that had not mattered; in the past her love of her work and the perks that went with it—free travel, the opportunity to meet new people, rent-free accommodation—had more than compensated for her smallish salary, but then in the past she had not had to worry about supporting anyone other than herself. In the past she had not had hanging over her the fact that her darling, beloved grandmother was soon going to be desperately in need of her help, not just financially but potentially physically as well.

Her employers had been very understanding, allowing her to terminate her employment with them without any notice—trust Gran not to let her know what was going on, not to want to worry her. It had been her GP—an old family friend—who had got in touch with Courage privately. Not even Gran knew the real extent of the damage to her heart and the frailty of her health.

'But there must be something you can do,' Courage had frantically protested to her grandmother's doctor, her body taut with shock and fear.

'Yes. We can operate to replace the damaged tissue, but the waiting-list for that kind of operation is at least two years. Your grandmother is a very strong woman, but she is in her sixties. Her condition is extremely severe, and another two years...'

Courage bit her lip. She couldn't bear the thought of losing her gran—or of seeing her in pain, suffering... Not Gran, who had always been so full of energy and optimism, who had been the steadfast rock of her own life, holding her close and safe, giving her the gift of self-worth, of knowing how much she was loved at a time when...

'What do you mean you've come home?' her grandmother had demanded when she had arrived unannounced. 'What about your work—your career?'

'Oh, that's all right,' Courage had fibbed breezily, fingers crossed behind her back. 'I had quite a bit of leave owing to me, and to be honest with you, Gran, I was already thinking about taking a break, giving myself some thinking time to evaluate where I'm going and what I want. The company have offered me the job of running their new Hong Kong conference centre and...'

'And what?' Her grandmother had demanded fiercely. 'It's the opportunity you've always wanted, what you've worked for...'

'In some ways,' Courage had agreed. 'And had it been anywhere else but Hong Kong they were posting me to...

After all, none of us are really sure what's going to happen when the colony is handed back to the Chinese.'

'So what exactly are you saying—that you turned them down?'

Courage had seen the suspicion in her grandmother's eyes, and knowing her pride, the same pride which she herself had inherited, she had broken one of her strongest rules and fibbed a second time.

'I haven't totally ruled it out. The company has given me three months to think it over.'

'Three months... But the longest you've ever been able to come home for before has been a couple of weeks.'

'Which is why I've got so much leave owing to me,' Courage had told her.

She had, of course, asked the doctor about a private operation for her grandmother, but when he had told her the cost her dismay must have shown in her face.

She knew that there was no way she could find the thousands of pounds it would cost for her grandmother's operation. The small cottage in which her grandmother lived was already mortgaged to the company which provided her with her pension annuity payments. Courage herself had no assets she could dispose of to raise any money, and there was no other family to go to.

Her father—her grandmother's only child—had died before Courage reached her teens, and her mother... Her mother, poor sad soul, had died in a swimming accident while on holiday with Courage's stepfather and his friends.

A small shudder passed through Courage's body, raising a rash of ominous goose-bumps on her flesh. Even now she hated thinking about her stepfather, about those years...

As she looked around the elegant, expensively furnished room in which she was sitting, with its silk curtains, its paintings and its antique furniture, she reflected that once she, too, had lived in surroundings as elegant as these.

Her stepfather's London house, while not as large as this beautiful Georgian mansion where she now sat so tensely in an ante-room waiting to be summoned for her interview, had certainly been equally as impressive, equally filled with expensive art treasures and antique furniture, all planned to awe and impress the poor dupes from whom her stepfather had earned his living, blinding them to the reality of what he really was with the rich luxury of his surroundings.

Fraud, the police had called it, but theft was what it really was. But her stepfather had escaped paying any price for his criminal activities, just as he had always escaped paying any price for anything he had done, for any of the lives he had destroyed.

The last time Courage had heard anything of him he had been living in Mexico, barred from re-entering the United States, where he had made his home after her mother's death.

No, there was no comparison between the lifestyle she had lived as a rich man's stepdaughter and that which she had known living with her grandmother in her small rural Dorset cottage. But there was no doubt, had never been any doubt in Courage's mind, which lifestyle she preferred... which home.

The last candidate for the job had been gone for a much longer time than any of the others, which didn't bode very well for her own chances, Courage acknowledged.

When the employment agency she had registered with had first contacted her about this job she had hardly been able to believe her luck.

'It isn't quite what you've been used to,' the woman who ran the agency had semi-apologised, 'and I suspect you could end up being more of a glorified housekeeper than anything else, but the salary is exceptionally high, transport is provided and you'd be working less than twenty miles away from where your grandmother lives.'

And she had gone on to explain the exact nature of the job in question and the requirements of her potential employer. Courage had found herself privately agreeing with the other woman's assessment of the situation.

The job description announced that her potential employer, an extremely wealthy businessman, wanted someone to take charge of the running of his country mansion. Duties would include organising various social and business functions, liaising with his staff in his London office, taking virtually full responsibility for the hiring and firing of staff at the house, and, on those occasions when he had foreign clients visiting him, organising any necessary business facilities for them, including interpreters etcetera.

Gideon Reynolds was the chairman and major stockholder of a complex network of high profit-earning enterprises, a conquistador of a man who had made his fortune and his name during the hectic times of the eighties, but who, unlike other less fortunate entrepreneurs, had gone on to build a very successful empire on the foundations of those successes.

Courage had, of course, researched as deeply as she could into his background and history once she had been told of the job, but had discovered frustratingly little about him. Even her grandmother, who knew all of the local gossip at every level, knew hardly anything about him, other than the fact that when he had first bought the house, which had been little more than an empty shell at the time, there had been a lot of semi-hysterical gossip locally that he planned to turn the house into some kind of leisure centre, complete with a huge golf course.

The leisure centre had never materialised; the golf course had—Gideon Reynolds apparently did a considerable amount of business with the Japanese, who enjoyed the pleasure of playing their favourite sport on a privately owned course.

Courage, who had worked in Japan herself for a while, could well appreciate what a clever move the golf course had been. Had he understood the basis of the Japanese male personality enough to institute such a move himself, or had he simply had very, very astute and knowledgeable advisers? she wondered.

The only thing she had been able to find out about him was that in addition to being a hugely wealthy man he was also extremely demanding to work for. Harsh-featured, ice-cold, merciless when it came to destroying an opponent—these were just some of the descriptions she had read of him in the financial press.

Disappointingly, none of the articles had contained any photographs of him. She knew he was somewhere in his early thirties, which made him six or seven years older than she was herself, and she knew that he wasn't married, that he had, in fact, never been married. Although there was no hint to be found anywhere that he was anything other than a thoroughly heterosexual male.

'Modern women do not appear to want marriage,' he had been quoted as saying in one article she had read—written, unsurprisingly, by a female financial correspondent. 'Or permanent commitment is not enough for them—they value sexual variety and expertise more than love and fidelity.'

'So you don't intend to marry?' the reporter had challenged him.

'One day. If only to ensure that I have someone to pass on the business to. But there is no urgency; a man, unlike a woman, can choose to become a parent virtually at any time in his adult life.'

'You're out of date,' the reporter had told him crisply. 'A woman can now opt to do the same...'

'Not my woman,' Gideon Reynolds had told her succinctly.

Another small shiver ran over Courage's skin as she recalled the article.

He didn't sound one little bit the sort of man she would have chosen to work for. Her mouth quirked slightly at the enormous mental understatement of her thoughts. But in this instance she had no choice.

If her time with Gran was going to be limited then she didn't want to waste a precious second of it. Not out of duty, because she thought it was what she owed her grandmother for all that she had done for her, but because she loved her... Loved her so much that already her heart was aching at the thought of losing her, of being alone.

As she blinked back the tears threatening to shadow her eyes—an unusual lavender-blue colour, which strangers always assumed meant she was wearing coloured contact lenses, but which, in fact, she had inherited from her grandmother, like her pale English rose complexion and her thick dark mane of Celtic curls—she focused on the huge oil-painting hanging on the wall above the marble Adam fireplace.

It was, she suspected, Italian. The subject matter was religious and allegorical, probably commissioned originally by some seventeenth-century English gentleman visiting Rome.

The walls of virtually every English stately home had at one time been decorated by such paintings, some of far more value than others. This, Courage suspected, was a particularly fine example of its genre; the impish expressions on the faces of the cherubs were so lifelike you could almost swear their eyes followed you, and as for the looks on the faces of the satyrs...

Was she being over-unfair as well as over-imaginative in considering their cynical, twisted smiles, their cold, calculating expressions as potentially mirroring those of the man who had bought and now owned them?

As he would own her if she came to work here. A small frown touched her forehead. It was so unlike her to be so over-imaginative, so very wary... So fearful, almost. Most people considered her to be a very controlled person, pleasantly self-confident and at ease in virtually any situation. She had learned long ago to control and conceal any kind of fear, and to know that to betray it was to give another person the potential power to hurt and damage. She prided herself in being fully in control of her own life, of being the kind of woman who made her own choices and her own decisions.

'Miss Bingham? Mr Reynolds will see you now.'

Smiling with a serenity she did not feel, Courage acknowledged the entrance of the male personal assistant who had opened the door, and who was watching her with admirable professional detachment as she stood up and walked towards him as he held the door open for her.

Presumably it was one of at least two doors into the boardroom beyond, since none of the previous candidates had returned to the ante-room following their interviews. Hopefully they *had* been allowed to leave, and had not been condemned to some deep, dank dungeon, having been verbally ripped apart by the sharp, predatory professional teeth of a man who, from the accounts she had read of him, more than lived up to his image of a less than friendly character.

Such flights of fantasy were so far removed from her normal calm, logical approach to life that Courage frowned slightly as she walked across the soft Aubusson carpet, noting as she did so that it had not been designed specially for the room, since its pattern did not follow the classic device of mirroring the plasterwork on the ceiling.

She was a tall woman—a fact which had led, in her teenage years, to people mistaking her for being much older than she was. Her bone-structure was slightly too slender for her height, causing people who did not know her well to dismiss her as vulnerable and fragile.

She was neither. Not now. Not since her grandmother had taught her how to be proud of herself and what she was. But she still cloaked the narrowness of her frame with clothes that matched her height—like the suit she was wearing today—so that instead of appearing fragile she gave the impression of strength and quiet power.

Men might find her slightly sexually intimidating, but if they were employers they also found it reassuring. No need to worry about having to mollycoddle a woman who stood five feet eleven in her stockinged feet and whose demeanour said that she was well able to cope with the hysterical tantrums of a temperamental chef or a bullying maitre d'.

She was, Courage noticed wryly as she walked past him, a good inch or so taller than the PA—a fact which she suspected he didn't very much like. She recognised the type. He would go for fluffy little blondes who made him feel good and who manipulated the hell out of him. He probably had a heavily dependent, immensely strong-willed mother somewhere, who clung to him with a stranglehold.

Courage gave him a calmly thoughtful look as she saw his glance drop to the front of her jacket.

'Thirty-six C,' she told him sweetly as she walked past him. 'Pretty much average for my height. It *was* on my application form. Along with the photograph that had been requested.'

She had balked a little at that, instinctively suspicious of any employer who needed to know what she looked like, but she had needed the job too much to refuse to supply such details.

The door did not open into a room, as she had imagined, but into a narrow panelled corridor without any windows. Walking down it made her feel mildly claustrophobic, a feeling she quickly quelled, in the same way that she refused to give in to the impulse to turn around and look at the PA as he followed her.

Some sixth sense made her pause outside the door at the end of the corridor to allow the PA to step past her and enter the room ahead of her, announcing her as he did so. After all, if she did get the job she would doubtless be working with him at times. She had let him know that there was no way she was going to be a walk-over; it was no stand-down on her part to acknowledge, and let him know that she acknowledged, his professional position.

'Miss Bingham.'

No lip-service here to political correctness with any use of the ubiquitous Ms. Not that Courage minded; she wasn't interested in the kind of respect that could be bought or earned with a title, and which was so often given grudgingly.

'Miss Bingham.'

As the man seated behind the massive Georgian partner's desk stood up, Courage only just managed to stop her mouth gaping open.

The board this man looked as though he should be impressing wasn't so much one of fellow directors and entrepreneurs but one run by the film censorship committee.

Courage couldn't remember ever, ever having seen such a sexually powerful and tauntingly male man.

Over the years her career had brought her into contact with very many good-looking men, and an equally large number of very wealthy men, but none, not one single one of them, had possessed a tenth of the open sexual charisma of this man.

She didn't like it, she decided, and she didn't like him either. She could almost feel the down-blast of the heat of his high testosterone levels, scent the intensely male pheromones which his body exuded like an invisible force-field.

Outwardly he was dressed in the familiar uniform of the successful businessman—an exclusively tailored suit, which disdained to advertise the handiwork of a fashionable designer but which had probably cost twice as much, a plain white shirt and an equally plain tie, a chrome watch on a leather strap and no rings or any other kind of jewellery. He had clean but unmanicured nails, thick dark hair, which was cut rather than styled, and skin which looked weathered rather than tanned and which was already beginning to show the beginnings of a five o'clock shadow.

That a man—any man—should possess such a high-octane brand of sexuality was disturbing enough; that he should so obviously choose not to acknowledge or underline it was...unsettling.

Good-looking men used their sexuality in just the same way as pretty women, but this man was making a positive visual statement that he did not choose to use his. Just because he didn't choose to, or because he didn't want to? He didn't look the sort, to Courage, who would have any difficulty in removing unattended, too-clinging female attachments from his life—no way.

'Please sit down.'

Courage discovered that she was rather glad to do so, and equally glad that the chair was positioned a good few yards away from the desk behind which he had re-seated himself.

'Courage. That's a rather unusual name.'

'It's a family name,' Courage explained calmly.

'I see from your application form that you describe yourself as single and unattached, and that you list your next of kin as your grandmother.'

'My parents are both dead,' Courage told him levelly. He had turned slightly away from her to study some papers on his desk, and as he did so something tugged at the corner of a vague memory, something about the angle of his jaw, the dark shadow he cast.

She was frowning, trying to ease the memory into something more concrete. It was like trying to ease a splinter out of a healed piece of skin. She could see it, feel it when she pressed the wound, but she could not extract it.

When the memory refused to take on any recognisable form she shook her head and let it go. It wasn't impossible that she had perhaps at some time caught a glimpse of him. He could quite easily have stayed in one of her hotels. She had certainly never seen him face to face; there was no way she would not have remembered him if she had. No, her memory was more something to do with the way he moved, the angle of his head, the...

'And you do not have any brothers...or sisters...?'

Courage tensed slightly as he seemed to hesitate over the last two words, giving them a very subtle underlining.

'No,' she told him curtly. 'My parents did not have any other children.'

That, at least, was the truth... And as for the rest... Well, a stepsister was not, after all, any real blood relation, and there had certainly never been any sisterly feelings between her and Laney. Contempt and hatred for Courage on Laney's part, and fear and loathing on her own.

Now that she was older the fear and loathing had gone, to be replaced by an enormous sense of sadness coupled with an equally intense sense of relief—and guilt... Guilt because she had escaped, because she had Gran, while Laney...

As a child she had only seen the closeness which existed between Laney and her father—Courage's own stepfather—as something which excluded her and threatened her relationship with her mother. Because her mother had done everything her second husband had told her, and Laney had tauntingly warned Courage that she was going to tell her father to send Courage away.

It was only later, as she grew more mature, that she had recognised the possible meaning of those nocturnal visits her stepfather had paid to Laney's room, the real foundation of the intense closeness which had existed between them.

She shuddered now to recall how easily she could have fallen into the same trap as her stepsister. Fortunately, she had been far too terrified of her stepfather to take him up on his offers to come to her room and 'talk' to her.

'Let me help sort out this problem you and Laney are having. You're sisters now and you should love each other. I *want* you to love each other,' he had insisted softly. 'Then I can love both of you. You mustn't quarrel with Laney, Courage. She's older than you. You must listen to her, let her help you.'

The cruel, manipulative nature of her stepsister, which had made her own early teen years such a misery, could, she acknowledged now, have been not so much a character defect as a direct result of the other girl's relationship with her father. Courage had no proof that he had been sexually abusive to Laney, but what she knew now as an adult, coupled with her own younger self's intuitive fear and distrust of the man, made her suspect that he could have been.

And her feelings were not just a whim, not just her jealousy over the way he had taken over her mother, shut Courage out; she was positive of that.

Her mother's second marriage was the one thing she and Gran never discussed. Her grandmother was of the old school and believed that if you couldn't say something good about a person then you shouldn't say anything at all.

Courage had been so shocked when she had heard the news of her mother's death, but in reality her true mother—the mother she had loved and who had loved her—had disappeared in the early months of her second marriage.

'No... I don't have any siblings,' she repeated firmly.

'No husband... No partner... No children.'

He was making statements rather than asking questions—after all, she had already supplied all that kind of information on the application form she had filled in, prior to being summoned for this interview—but Courage still responded as though he were questioning her.

'Isn't that rather unusual... in these days?'

Courage focused on him. What was he implying? That she was lying—concealing the truth? Or did his question go deeper, probing the foundations of the most personal aspects of herself?

'Unusual, but not unknown... Not in the hotel trade,' she responded calmly.

It was, after all, true. The hours she worked and the constant travelling were just two of the reasons why it wouldn't have been easy for her to form a close, emotional, sexual relationship with a man; up until she had moved back to her grandmothers her 'home' had been a room in whatever hotel complex the company had posted her to, and her 'commitment' had been the major and most important commitment in her life—the one she had made to her career. But when it had come to making a choice between that career and her grandmother...

Her employers had told her that if she should change her mind at some stage in the future they would be more than happy to welcome her back, and had in fact pleaded with her not to go—especially Gunther, the eldest son of the Swiss family who owned the hotel chain.

'It says on your application form that you left your previous post for personal reasons.'

'Yes,' Courage agreed. 'I wanted to return to England to be with my grandmother, who is suffering from a...heart condition. She...she brought me up when...when my mother remarried and I...'

'You what? You feel you owe it to her to repay what she did for you? That's a very old-fashioned ideology, if I may say so.'

'I'm a very old-fashioned person,' Courage responded coolly, sensing the cynicism behind his words. 'But in actual fact no, it isn't duty that brought me back. I happen to love my grandmother and I *want* to be with her. Left to her own devices, she's all too likely to take on too much...to overtax herself and——'

'Is her condition treatable?'

'There *is* an operation, but the waiting-list is very long and she isn't a priority case. Private treatment is out of the question, but if Gran can be persuaded to take things easy, preserve her strength...'

'You do realise that you're vastly over-qualified for this job, don't you?'

'I need to earn my living...'

'Well, you certainly won't earn much of one stacking supermarket shelves... Certainly not enough to pay for the kind of outfit you're wearing right now. Chanel, isn't it?'

'A copy. I had it made when I took a business trip to Hong Kong,' Courage corrected him gently. 'Hotel management doesn't pay anything like enough to buy Chanel.'

She had intended the words only as a small rebuke, a subtle warning that his comments were not either welcome or necessary, but the long, thorough look he gave her coupled with his laconic, 'No, it doesn't,' made the hot, angry colour sting her skin.

There were a variety of ways of interpreting his remarks, none of them particularly charitably inclined towards herself, and all of them variations on a theme. It was pretty obvious, she decided, that she was not going to get the job.

Without saying as much, Gideon Reynolds was giving her the distinct impression that he was trying to get under her skin and manoeuvre her into some kind of angry outburst with his subtle insults. Why, she had no idea. Perhaps he was just that kind of man, and that was the way he liked to enjoy himself. Well, if he did that was his problem, but there was no way she was going to allow him to manipulate her.

As she waited for him to dismiss her and tell her that the interview was over she was frantically trying to work out how many part-time jobs—working behind bars, stacking supermarket shelves and doing whatever else might come along—she could find the time and the energy to take on. At the moment...

'How does your grandmother feel about the fact you've given up your career to come home and look after her?'

His question surprised Courage into looking directly at him, something she had been very careful not to do, she recognised unwillingly. His eyes were flint-grey, hard like the coldest northern seas, threatening that immense danger could lurk beneath their deceptively calm surface.

'She doesn't know. She thinks I've taken an extended holiday to think about my future career path. That I may give up my international job because I don't want a permanent position in Hong Kong.'

She saw the way his eyebrows lifted and gave a small mental shrug to herself. She had already as good as lost the job; she might as well tell him the truth.

'Aren't you worried that someone might tell her the truth?'

'No, why should I be? Besides, no one knows,' Courage admitted.

The friends she had made locally as a girl had either moved away now, to pursue their own careers, or were married with young, demanding children—far too busy to question deeply what she was doing. And as for worrying her grandmother by telling her... Why should they do so? Her grandmother was a very well-liked person—a very well-loved person.

'And if you don't get this job, what then? Back to filling supermarket shelves?'

He seemed to have a thing about that; perhaps because he considered it was the kind of work he would never demean himself by doing. Well, she didn't consider it demeaning—far from it.

'There are far worse ways of earning a living,' she pointed out fiercely. 'And, as far as I am concerned, the kind of people who consider honest, physical labour something demeaning, something to be mocked, are just not worth knowing.'

Well, she really had burned her bridges now, Courage acknowledged, to judge from the look he was giving her, but she didn't care. In her book the kind of people who were really to be despised were like her stepfather—outwardly publicly fêted, and acclaimed, well-respected businessmen, who in reality were little more than thieves, preying on the vulnerability and, yes, sometimes the ignorant material greed of others. For all she knew, Gideon Reynolds, too, could be like them. Outwardly lauded and respected but inwardly, secretly...

It was true there had been nothing in the financial press to suggest that his business success was based on anything other than flair and nerve; nothing to say that he had prospered through the same kind of fraudulent dishonesty as her stepfather. But there was still something about him that made her almost glad that she was not going to get the job. A sense of...not fear, exactly... More...more apprehension ... A feeling of being mentally circled by the mind of a predator.

Nervously she licked her lips. Now she was letting his overwhelming male sexuality cause her imagination to run wild, but even if she dismissed the discomfort there was still something intimidating and unnerving about the man which, coupled with that irritatingly elusive flicker of recognition, made her feel not just wary and on edge. It was as though...as though...

'How much would it cost for your grandmother to have her operation privately?'

Courage stared at him, a small frown pleating her forehead. Why was he asking her so many questions on a subject which could surely be of only limited interest to him?

'Her GP wasn't specific. There wasn't really any need,' Courage hedged.

There *hadn't* really been any need. Once he'd told Courage what the minimum cost of the operation would be she had known there was simply no way she could finance it. She had *some* savings, a small nest-egg, but nothing more.

'How much?' she was asked a second time, the male voice which so far had been unexpectedly soft for so formidable a man suddenly sharpening and hardening, betraying just a hint of the high-octane power its owner could potentially release when necessary.

'Upwards of ten thousand pounds,' Courage told him quietly, swallowing down the huge lump of anxious despair that filled her throat every time she thought of the vast sum of money which stood between her grandmother and good health.

'Ten thousand... Umm... Not an impossible sum for someone to raise these days... Presumably your grandmother owns her own home and——?'

'Yes, but she has already used it to purchase an annuity,' Courage interrupted him.

She had had enough of his questions. She had come here to be interviewed for a job—a job she was one hundred and ten per cent certain she was not going to get.

'And you have no one... no family... no connections who could help?'

'No, no one,' Courage told him angrily.

The very thought of asking either Laney or her stepfather for help of any kind—even if she had known where to contact them—made her mouth curl in a bitterly painful smile. Her stepfather had hated her grandmother, had tried every trick in the book to persuade her mother to change her mind about allowing her grandmother to take charge of Courage and to get her back under his own roof, but fortunately her mother had stood firm.

Courage had often wondered in the years since she herself had grown up if her grandmother had perhaps guessed, sensed in some way the danger her daughter-in-law's second marriage had posed to Courage. Courage's mother had been a pretty, fragile woman, who had liked parties and socialising. The kind of woman that these days it seemed impossible to believe had ever existed; the kind of woman who needed a man in her life to 'look after her'.

A discreet tap on the door heralded the arrival of the PA.

'I'm sorry to disturb you,' he apologised to his boss. 'Sir Malcolm will be arriving shortly. The 'copter pilot has just radioed in to say they'll be landing on time.'

'Yes, thank you, Chris.'

As Gideon Reynolds started to stand up, Courage did the same. Her interview was obviously at an end, and no doubt all those unexpected and unwelcome questions about her grandmother had simply been a means of idling away a few spare minutes of time before his visitor arrived. Well, she hoped it had amused him to see how the other half lived, Courage decided angrily.

No doubt the ten thousand pounds that was so unobtainable to her that it might as well have been ten million was something he probably spent in a weekend, entertaining a girlfriend. More, she decided sourly, since he was obviously such an expert on Chanel couture clothes. But not such an expert that he had recognised that hers was a copy.

'Tell me, Miss Bingham,' she heard him asking unexpectedly, 'what would you do if you were anticipating the arrival of a VIP and you learned from the helicopter pilot that not only was he late picking up his passenger but that the reason he was late was because the machine was being serviced when he arrived to fly it? Your VIP guest, by the way, is a rather irascible person, who has only agreed to attend the meeting you have arranged on the understanding that he will not be kept waiting.'

'Initially I would recall the helicopter—no appointment, no meeting, no matter how essential, is so important that someone's life should be put at risk, and if the machine was still in the process of being serviced there would be no guarantee that it would not develop some sort of problem. I would then contact the passenger, apologise for the delay and assure him that he would be picked up within fifteen minutes.'

She saw the way his eyebrows rose and added, with more self-assurance than she actually felt, 'If he was being collected from a helicopter pad then it would have to be within range of a national helicopter service. I would obtain a substitute machine and pilot from my own contacts—if I regularly used helicopter transport I would, of course, already know of a reliable back-up service. I would make sure I was on hand the moment the VIP arrived, with both an apology and an explanation, and I would follow this up later, having first of all made sure that he was still able to leave at the originally stated time.'

'And the original cause of the delay, the mistimed service, how would you deal with that?'

'That would depend on whether or not I was responsible for its mistiming...'

'And if you were?'

'I wouldn't be,' Courage told him crisply. 'Because I would have already made sure that the machine was ready for the pilot to collect at the stated time—and if it wasn't I would have had a substitute serviced machine there for him.'

'Very efficient.'

'I try to be...'

He was already walking over to the door and Courage followed him, coming to an abrupt halt as, unexpectedly, he turned round.

There was less than a metre between them...

She had already seen that he was tall—at least six feet four since she had had to look up at him—and that the physique beneath his subtly tailored jacket possessed the kind of powerful muscle-structure that no desk-bound man could ever possibly have. This man worked out in a gym and he played sport—to win, Courage suspected, and roughly.

Through the polar whiteness of his cotton shirt she could actually see the dark shadow of his body hair. A small shudder ran through her, heat zigzagging through her body like lightning, searing along her cheekbones. She could feel her face burning with mortification as he looked at her.

There had been a time in her life when the sight of a bare male chest covered in body hair had been enough to make her want to curl up and die with embarrassed, shocked awareness of such sexuality—and her own reaction to it. But that had been a long time ago and she had got over it... Just as she had got over...other things.

'What's wrong?'

'N-n-n-nothing,' Courage lied. 'I——'

'Don't you want to know whether or not you have got the job?'

He was playing with her, taunting her. Angry sparks flashed in Courage's eyes.

'You said yourself that I was over-qualified for it.'

'Which means that I'd be a fool not to snap you up, doesn't it? When can you start?'

As she fought to control the jumble of confused thoughts and emotions stampeding wildly through her, Courage was still aware of her apparent new employer's watchful scrutiny of her. It was as though he was looking for some kind of specific reaction, the angle of his head, his jawline as he studied her... The angle of his head?

She frowned, desperately trying to catch hold of the tail-end of the vague wisp of dark memory which still eluded her. It was no use, it was gone. But she had the job, and that was what she ought to be concentrating on right now, not some uncomfortable feeling that there was something somehow familiar to her about her new boss.

Familiar but not familiar-pleasant, or even familiar-indifferent, she acknowledged half an hour later as she drove home in her grandmother's ancient Morris. No, the kind of familiarity which had stirred so elusively through her was the kind that carried with it uncomfortable feelings of fear and anxiety.

Frowning, Courage changed gear for a sharp bend. There was no point in worrying about it. Wherever it was she had seen him before it would come back to her sooner or later. And, after all, she didn't have to like the man; she simply had to work for him.

Ideally, he might not be her choice of employer, but that was hardly important; what *was* important was being able to be close to her grandmother. She was only sixty-seven—not old at all, really—and if Courage could just persuade her to take things more easily until she could have the operation...

The salary Gideon Reynolds had offered her had been astonishingly generous, far more than she had been earning—when he had mentioned the figure he would be paying her her mouth had dropped slightly.

'What's wrong?' he had asked her. 'Isn't it as much as you already earn?'

'It's more,' Courage had told him honestly—and had caught the quickly suppressed flicker of surprise in his own eyes. 'It seems a lot to pay someone for the amount of work involved.'

'A good workman is always worthy of his hire,' Gideon had responded smoothly. 'And I promise you won't find that the job is any sinecure.'

'I shouldn't want to,' Courage had countered promptly.

What was it about the man that made her feel as though he was constantly challenging her, constantly probing...? Constantly testing her, almost...

As she turned off the main road and into the lane which led to her grandmother's cottage her frown deepened. Why had Gideon Reynolds been so surprised by her honesty? Surely he wouldn't have employed her if he had felt that he couldn't trust her?

Stop worrying about him, she advised herself mentally, and start worrying instead about what Gran's going to say when she hears your news.

CHAPTER TWO

'YOU'VE done what? But why? You've always said how much you love your job... The travel, meeting different people, the——'

'Yes, I know, Gran, but things have changed,' Courage told her, frowning as she saw the small set of step-ladders standing next to the large old-fashioned dresser which dominated one wall of her grandmother's kitchen.

'What are those doing there?' she demanded accusingly.

'What does it look like? It's time that dresser had a good clean. The awful weather stopped me getting on with my usual spring cleaning, and it's high time I got down to it...'

'Gran, you haven't been climbing those steps? You know what the specialist said,' Courage scolded her worriedly.

'Yes, I know,' her grandmother agreed grimly. 'But if you think I'm going to spend the rest of my days being wrapped in cotton wool and treated like a semi-invalid... I've got a minor heart condition, that's all...'

If only that were the case.

'And if you think I'm going to let you give up your job because of me...'

'I'm not,' Courage was quick to reassure her, mentally crossing her fingers as she added untruthfully, 'The hotel trade has been hit very badly by the recession, Gran. I didn't want to say anything before and worry you but... Well, there's been a lot of talk about enforced redundancies...'

'Is that why you got that part-time job at the supermarket?' her grandmother questioned her.

'Yes,' Courage told her. Originally she had told her grandmother that her three-month stay with her would be too much for both of them if they spent every second in one another's company, and that her part-time job would give them both a bit of space.

'This new job will give me a chance to broaden my experience. I'll be in full charge of the organisation of the household for all his social and business events. Apparently, one of the reasons he bought the estate was to use it for business purposes; his Japanese customers in particular enjoy that kind of thing.'

'What is his business, exactly?' her grandmother asked her.

'His company designs parks and gardens on a large scale rather than a small one. You know the kind of thing—municipal open spaces, hotel grounds, atriums. He does a lot of business in the Middle East—especially Kuwait. Apparently he's an expert in "greening" arid areas, and his assistant was telling me that he's been consulted by the authorities in Australia and California following the fires they've had there. He has an office in London but apparently he's presently in the process of moving everything down here.'

'Mmm... Well, from what I've heard he's an extremely shrewd businessman, and very single-minded when it comes to getting what he wants. When does he want you to start work?'

'Next Monday. I've got an appointment with him on Friday afternoon to sign my contract of employment and go over the way he wants me to work. Apparently he's flying out to New York on Monday morning, so he won't be there, and he won't be back until later in the week.'

'Mmm... Well, if you're sure it's what you want...'

'I'm sure,' Courage told her firmly.

It was just as well she had left herself plenty of extra time to make the appointment, Courage acknowledged wryly, as the Morris had stubbornly refused to start. She had had to ring for a taxi and then book the Morris into the garage for a service. It was just as well that a car was one of the perks of her new job.

She noticed that Chris Elliott's smile was only slightly warmer as the PA opened the front door to her.

'He's in the study waiting for you,' he told Courage. 'His new Californian appointment has been brought forward. Congratulations on getting the job, by the way.'

'Thank you.' Courage responded to his smile with one of her own—one of equally tepid warmth.

From what Gideon Reynolds had told her her job ran parallel to Chris's, not either below or above it, but she suspected that the PA would try to manoeuvre himself into a slightly superior position to her if he thought he could. She had no wish to get involved in any kind of power struggle with him, but neither was she going to allow him to manipulate her.

It was a warm spring day, and Courage had opted for a slightly more casual but still businesslike outfit than the one she had had on for her initial interview: a soft, spotted silk culotte suit, in brown with cream spots, and a toning cream short-sleeved jacket. Like her 'Chanel', she had had it made in Hong Kong.

As she knocked briefly on the half-open study door, and then walked in on Gideon's command, she noticed him looking briefly at her legs in an automatic male reflex gesture. Nothing was particularly personal in the brief look he gave her, but nevertheless it made her wish she had worn a longer skirt—and tights. Not because of his look but because of her own reaction to it. She was acutely conscious of the tiny frisson of unwanted sensation that ran quickly across her skin.

'Please sit down,' Gideon commanded her. 'I'm afraid I don't have a lot of time. My Californian appointment has been brought forward and I'm flying out tonight instead of on Monday. Here's a copy of your contract. If you'd like to read through it...'

Dutifully Courage took the document from him, reading it as quickly as she could. She had just got to the bottom of the penultimate page when she stopped abruptly, lifting her head in astonishment.

'What's this?' she demanded uncertainly. 'You didn't say anything about making me a loan of ten thousand pounds when you interviewed me.'

'I didn't think about it until after you'd gone,' Gideon told her dismissively. 'In fact, it wasn't until I was drawing up the contract that it occurred to me that by advancing you a part of your salary it would enable you to arrange for your grandmother's operation.'

'Advancing *part* of my salary?' Courage protested. 'But...'

'If you read on you'll see that the contract covers a two-year period with five thousand being deducted from each year's salary to repay the loan, which will be interest-free as it is as much in my interest as it is your own.'

'As much in *your* interest?' Courage's forehead creased, pleated in a small frown. 'I'm sorry, but I just don't understand how...'

'As you'll soon discover, once you start working for me, I demand one hundred and twenty per cent concentration all day, every day from my employees... That's what I pay them for. I do not want their minds wandering to personal matters while they're supposed to be concentrating on their work. Therefore, it makes sense to do all that I can to ensure that their minds do not have cause to wander. It's obvious from what you told me that you are extremely concerned about your grandmother's health—to the point, I suspect, where there could be occasions when your concern for her could have a detrimental effect on your work. And that is something I do not want.'

'But you said nothing about offering me a loan when you offered me the job,' Courage protested, still not totally able to take in what she had just read.

'Simply because at the time it hadn't occurred to me. However, if you feel you'd prefer not to take it, I can...'

'No, no, of course not... I...I'm very grateful to you for... It has come as such a shock... I wasn't expecting...'

To Courage's embarrassment she could feel her eyes suddenly starting to fill with tears as her throat closed up with emotion.

It was just beginning to dawn on her what Gideon Reynold's offer of a loan would mean. Her grandmother could have her operation; her life would no longer be in jeopardy. And she would have to remain here working for Gideon Reynolds for the next two years.

Courage frowned. Why should that knowledge daunt her? She knew she was up to the job—more than up to it... So what was it that bothered her? And something did, she knew that from the small sinking feeling which had followed her initial sense of stunned relief. Was it the man himself, Gideon Reynolds who daunted her? But why? Why should he?

She had come across powerful, egocentric men before—plenty of them. She had come across sexually magnetic men before, as well. Yes, but none of them had been quite so... None of them had been... None of them had caused that small, shocking quiver of sexual sensation which had raced through her when she had seen Gideon Reynolds looking at her legs. Was that what she was trying to tell herself?

Oh, come on, she derided herself mentally. He caught you off-guard, that's all. He looked, you responded—that's all. It doesn't mean anything. Not to you and certainly not to him.

She could see Gideon flicking back his cuff and glancing frowningly at his watch, a none too subtle reminder to her that he was in a hurry.

She looked back down at the contract. Ten thousand pounds. It would be enough to cover the cost of Gran's operation, and with the rest of her salary there would be something to provide for her recuperation. She'd been a complete idiot even to think of not accepting. For Gran's sake, as well as her own.

It was just that it had come as such a shock and she had been so unprepared, she decided ten minutes later as she handed her signed contract back to Gideon. That was why, instead of feeling euphoric and overjoyed, she felt oddly tense and anxious.

She didn't like having surprises sprung upon her, even pleasant ones. Just as she didn't like being in situations over which she did not have at least some control. No doubt an analyst would tell her that her apprehension, her fear, sprang from the time of her mother's second marriage.

'Good. I've got the cheque here for you.'

Shakily Courage focused on Gideon Reynolds' face as he reached into a drawer at the side of his desk and removed a cheque.

Three things struck her as he handed it to her, all of them slightly disturbing. The first was that the cheque was drawn on his personal account, the second that he had obviously been sure enough of her acceptance to have had it made out already, and the third that there was something almost gloating in the unexpectedly brilliant gleam of his eyes as he handed the cheque over to her.

Just for a moment Courage had the oddest impulse to hand it back to him, to tell him that she had changed her mind. What if their working relationship didn't work out and she was committed to a two-year contract and no way of paying the loan back? But she found herself accepting the cheque, smiling her thanks and pushing her worries to the back of her mind.

'I shall be leaving shortly, but Chris will show you round the house so that you can familiarise yourself with its lay-out. I shall be returning from California on Wednesday, if all goes to plan. On Thursday evening I shall be holding a dinner party for twenty or so guests, some of whom will be staying overnight. Chris will fill you in with all the details. Oh, and I've also given him instructions to arrange for a couple of cars to be delivered for you to test-drive.'

Without realising she had been doing so, Courage had been playing with the chain on the small seed-pearl locket which hung around her neck. Her father had given it to her mother as an engagement present, and when she had gone to live with her grandmother her mother had given it to her. Courage wore it all the time and a small, distressed protest left her lips as the chain suddenly snapped under the pressure of her nervous fingers, the locket spinning across the desk towards Gideon Reynolds.

Courage reached out to retrieve it, but Gideon moved faster, covering it, stopping its escape with his hands just seconds ahead of her, so that it was impossible for her to stop the downward movement of her own fingers which brought them on top of his.

Immediately she was aware of the male warmth of his flesh. It made her own skin tingle in shocked awareness of the tremendous physical power in the lean strength of his fingers. Her own hand looked tiny against his, her flesh so much paler and softer. The tingle became a hot, fast burn.

A pulse suddenly started to beat very rapidly in her throat, her face flushing in a sudden surge of sexual heat so shocking and unexpected that it was several betraying seconds before she could respond to it and snatch her fingers from his, breaking the magnetic contact. She had not felt so physically aware of a man since——

Fresh colour burned her face—caused by embarrassment this time—as she recognised what she was feeling and immediately tried to suppress it. Such an instant and overwhelming physical reaction to a man was totally out of character for her. She was normally very cautious, even wary with men in the sexual sense. Her libido was something she had never previously had any problem whatsoever in controlling. And Gideon Reynolds wasn't even her kind of man, really. He was far too sexy, far too potently male; that raw, sexual energy he possessed was something she would have expected to repel her, reminding her as it did of her past and all the pain it held.

Discomfort scorched her face as she tried to avoid looking directly at him. Thank heavens she still had her jacket on and he couldn't see the betraying thrust of her breasts beneath it. It was crazy for her body to start reacting to him like this, impossible... She barely knew him... Didn't like him... Had never been attracted to power, in any of its forms, and...

'A gift from a man?' she heard him questioning as he reached over to her to hand the locket back to her. 'A man', he had said, but 'a lover' was what he had meant, Courage recognised.

'It... belonged to my mother... My father gave it to her...' she told him jerkily, too dismayed by her reaction to him to preserve her normal reticence.

'Well, it looks like you're going to need a new chain for it... I doubt that this one can be repaired.'

Courage flinched, and totally unexpectedly he reached out and touched the broken chain. She could feel his knuckles brushing against her throat, his thumb resting against the frantic pulse that raced there. Panic flooded through her. He was looking right at her, straight into her eyes, and there was no way that she could look away from him.

Slowly his gaze dropped to her mouth and stayed there. The flesh of her lips felt unbearably hot, and so dry that she longed to touch them with her tongue, to soften and moisten them. She was breathing far too shallowly, panting almost, and beneath the fabric of her top she could feel the hard thrust of her nipples where the silk rasped as delicately against them as the tip of a lover's tongue.

Courage shuddered visibly, her eyes unwittingly betraying her, shocked at her own thoughts. She couldn't move, say or do anything as she felt Gideon's finger brush delicately against her skin, as though he was going to slide his hand against her throat. His thumbtip stroked the sensitive flesh behind her ear as he angled her head backwards, as if he would kiss her—his lips sensitising her mouth in the same way that his fingertips were sensitising her skin, his tongue-tip stroking over them, his lips then probing them, his teeth taking hungry, fierce lover's bites at her mouth, devouring her, while his hands...

'Your chain. If you leave it dangling there like that you'll lose it...'

Courage froze as she felt him move away from her and saw the golden glitter of her broken chain as he slid it through his fingers. Humiliation washed over her in a scarlet tide. What on earth had she been thinking? Had she totally taken leave of her senses?

Thank God Gideon Reynolds couldn't read her mind, see what she had been thinking and feeling. She felt almost sick with shock and disbelief. She had never been guilty of that kind of sexual fantasising before—not even about an imaginary lover, never mind a man who was all too real and very, very much too male for her cautious taste.

It must be the shock of him offering her the loan; something to do with the relief of not having to worry so much about her grandmother any longer. Some kind of peculiar mental and physical reaction to the release of stress and anxiety. Hastily Courage seized on this explanation for her behaviour with shaky relief.

Yes, that was it. Her body was just reacting to the release of all the recent tension and fear. That was all. That was all... And that *would* be all, she told herself firmly as Gideon Reynolds walked over to the door and held it open for her.

'Until next week, then, and, in the interim, if there should be any problem Chris will——'

'There won't be any problems,' Courage assured him firmly, determined to dispel any impression she might just have given him that she couldn't be trusted to behave either professionally or competently.

'I hope not.'

Dulcet though his voice was, there was no mistaking his warning.

CHAPTER THREE

WHEN she had made that statement she had reckoned without a chef who had given his immediate notice and walked out within hours of her taking up her new post, Courage admitted grimly as the irate Italian refused to allow her to placate him and departed to pack his bags.

The cause of his dissatisfaction was apparently a mixture of things, chief of which, so far as Courage could discern, was hurt pride at Gideon Reynolds' apparent uninterest in allowing him to show off his culinary talents by never providing a sufficiently appreciative number of dinner guests.

'I am master chef, but not once have I been allowed to show this. It is all single dinners, working lunches, healthy breakfasts. That is not what I spend ten years training for.'

'But Alfonso, all that is going to change...'

'It is too late,' Alfonso had told her angrily. 'I do not cook healthy breakfasts...working lunches...single dinners,' he had recited with a contemptuous curl of his lips. 'I am a chef... I create meals which are a work of art—a delight to the connoisseur's taste-buds, a feast for the discerning.'

Courage knew when she was fighting a losing battle.

'No luck with Alfonso?' Chris commiserated. 'The boss isn't going to be too pleased to come back and find him gone.'

Courage had already decided that on a personal note she was never going to like Gideon's PA, but professionally it was just as much her job to ensure that they could work well together as it was to find a replacement for Alfonso. And so she ignored the malicious pleasure which accompanied his comment.

'You know why he's bought this place, don't you?' Chris continued cynically, ignoring the fact that Courage had returned her attention to her own work and quite plainly did not wish to discuss the subject.

'It's obvious what he's up to,' Chris added contemptuously, when Courage refused to make any response. 'They're all the same, these self-made millionaire types. They all try to do it, don't they, one way or another? Use their wealth to try and buy themselves a place in society. First the country house, then the attempts to buy or bribe their way into local society, followed by marriage to a suitably upper class and impoverished bride. It's the classic way to do it, isn't it? The final touch to their success, their entry ticket into the otherwise closed ranks of the upper classes. Not that it ever works. Oh, they think they've succeeded, but they are never properly accepted...not really.'

As she heard the contemptuous satisfaction in his voice Courage's resolve not to be drawn into conversation with him deserted her, and her eyes flashed angrily as she asked him coldly, 'Don't you think that sort of attitude is rather out of date these days—*and* out of place? Gideon *is*, after all, our employer.'

'Oh, so that's the way the wind's blowing, is it?' Chris countered mockingly. 'Well, you're wasting your time entertaining any hopes in that direction. Oh, you might make it as far as his bed,' he told Courage nastily, 'but if you were thinking of something more permanent— like a wedding-ring on your finger—you don't stand a chance. You haven't got the right background, don't you see? Now if, for instance, you had a father or an uncle who was a member of the landed gentry or, even better, a member of the aristocracy, you might be in with a chance...'

The venom in his voice shocked Courage a little. Some of it, she knew, was directed against her, but most of it was not for her but for Gideon Reynolds. She could well understand a man like this being a little envious of him— he was, after all, a hugely successful and rich man, and men were notorious for their competitiveness and jealousy in such arenas—but that still didn't explain why she instinctively felt compelled to defend their absent employer.

She said quietly, 'I'm sure you're wrong. After all, if Gideon wanted a title with his wealth I'm sure he could find a way of buying himself one.'

'Oh, no doubt. A charity peerage. But you see those are ten a penny, and that would not open the kind of doors he wants to have opened, no matter how much it might impress the peasantry. Why do you think he bought this place? Not just because it will make a convenient showplace for his clients. Oh, no, it's what they all do, you see... First the millions, then the stately pile and the aristocratic wife, then the mongrel brats who'll have their names put down for all the best schools. Of course, once they are there they'll soon end up despising their father and——'

'Since you obviously dislike him so much I'm surprised you go on working for him,' Courage interrupted him. She was beginning to get angry now, her eyes flashing her feelings.

'I don't have any option—you see *my* father wasn't rich. Do you know what old Gideon was before he became a millionaire? He was a labourer, paid by the day.'

'There's nothing wrong with that,' Courage told him fiercely. She could remember her stepfather voicing very much the same views, his voice soft with cruel contempt.

'My dear Courage, you should be grateful to me for providing you with such a beautiful home,' he had told her. 'Unlike your late father. He, I understand, was never very good with money. However, it seems you are not grateful. In fact, you are becoming extremely disruptive, upsetting my daughter and your mother. I've been having a word with your mother and we both feel that a year or so at boarding-school will probably help you to be more appreciative.'

Courage had said nothing, simply standing there, white-faced and sick with misery.

'You'll be sorry,' Laney had warned her viciously after their quarrel. 'I'm going to get my father to send you away—to boarding-school.'

'You can't . . . My mother won't let you,' Courage had protested. But she had been wrong.

In the end, though, as she had discovered, there were far worse things in life than boarding-school, and in fact, once she had got over missing her mother, she had actually begun to enjoy the relative peace and quiet of a life with no Laney in it.

'No? Oh, I see, you're the type who gets turned on by the thought of a bit of rough trade, are you? You like the idea of being mauled about by some beefy labourer with grimy hands and broken nails, the kind who——'

Anger flashed fiercely in Courage's eyes as she interrupted Chris again.

'Your prejudices and your views on our mutual employer are your own affair, and nothing to do with me. I'm here to work—we both are—so if you'll excuse me, that is exactly what I am going to do.'

She would have liked to say more, but there was no point in deliberately antagonising the man. What she couldn't understand was why on earth Gideon Reynolds employed him. Surely he must be aware of what kind of person he was, or of what kind of views he held—he was far, far too intelligent not to be. Still, that was Gideon's problem and not hers—thankfully.

So Gideon would only marry a society woman, Courage mused half an hour later as she searched through her personal organiser for the telephone number she wanted—a London-based employment agency which specialised in supplying catering staff.

Over the years Courage had built up her own private store of such numbers—contacts she could rely on, agencies all over the world who she knew from personal experience were the best in their field. It was part of her job to have that kind of knowledge, those kinds of contacts at her fingertips; it was one of the things which had made her into the professional that she now was. She had known, without vanity, that when her Swiss employers had protested that they did not want to lose her they had been speaking the truth.

She knew they had valued her professionalism and her loyalty, just as she valued the training and support they had given her. But, as she had explained to them, when it came to making a choice between her career and her grandmother, there really was no contest.

Her frown deepened, her hand hovering over the telephone. Why should the talk about Gideon Reynolds getting married, becoming the property of another woman, disturb her so much? It ought to make her feel just the opposite. Previously she had always preferred to work for and with men who were obviously and openly happily married. So much so in fact, that the other girls she had worked with had often teased her about it. There had been, after all, no point in her trying to explain that she felt happier that way... safer...

By the end of the afternoon she had managed to solve one of her problems. The agency had managed to find her a replacement chef—a woman who had trained under the Roux brothers and who was currently between jobs. Courage arranged to travel to London to interview her.

The other major problem, which had been on her mind for most of the day, would not be quite so easily solved, she acknowledged as she replaced the telephone receiver.

Her grandmother, far from passively accepting her announcement that Courage wanted to use her 'savings' to pay for her grandmother to have her operation done privately, had instantly and suspiciously demanded to know why Courage was so anxious to bundle her into hospital for an operation which would cost the earth when, if she waited a couple of years, she could have it done anyway.

'Two years is the minimum waiting time,' Courage had argued craftily. 'It could be longer, and you know that Dr Howard says you've got to take things easy until you've had it done.'

Both Courage and Dr Howard were agreed that her grandmother should not be worried or frightened by being told how very serious her condition was.

'You mean, if I haven't had it done by the time I'm seventy then I could be judged too old to have it done at all?' her grandmother had suggested.

'Well, it does happen,' Courage had pointed out, but she had had to bite her lip and turn away so that her grandmother couldn't see the look in her eyes and guess how very real was the possibility of her not being able to live long enough to have her operation.

'Well, that's as maybe,' her grandmother had countered, changing tack, 'but I am not having you wasting your savings on me... And besides——' she had started to frown '—I do know how much this operation will cost, you know. You haven't got that kind of money, Courage.'

'Yes, I have,' Courage had told her, willing the betraying colour not to run up under her skin as she fibbed. 'I... There was some money after... after mother died. I... I never mentioned it at the time...'

'Some money... Whose money?' her grandmother had demanded suspiciously. 'Your mother didn't *have* any money, and if you think I'm going to let you pay for that operation with that man's money, then...'

She had looked gravely at her grandmother. 'Do you think I could ever bring myself to touch a penny of his?' Tears had filled Courage's eyes and her grandmother had reached out and patted her hand.

'I'm sorry, love... It's just... Well, it's just my silly pride, I suppose. It seems all wrong, somehow, you having to spend your money on me.'

'Who better to spend it on? You're all I've got, Gran.'

'Well, yes. And that's another thing—you should be married, Courage... You should have children of your own to worry about...'

'Are you trying to tell me that I'm on the shelf and past it?' Courage had teased, trying to lighten the emotional atmosphere.

'What I'm trying to tell you is that life can be lonely without someone of your own to share it with. I loved your grandfather very much. When he was killed during the war... Well, I had your father to think of, and then you, but we all need someone to love, Courage, and someone to be loved by.'

Courage fully agreed. The problem for her was finding that special someone—and they would have to be special. Her mother's second marriage had left Courage wary. She liked men as friends, enjoyed their company and their conversation, but when it came to anything more intimate, Courage recognised uncomfortably now, as she dipped her head and started to twiddle with her hair, how very betraying her body language was.

She wasn't just unhappy about the reality of total and emotional intimacy with a man, she was ill at ease even thinking about it. Not because she found the thought of sex unappealing, or frightening in any way. No, it wasn't that that made her want to close her mind against her own thoughts, to shut them out and ignore them—in the same way that she had been fiercely trying to ignore the effect which Gideon's touch had had on her ever since that small incident in his study—it was...

It was guilt that made her feel this way, she admitted. The guilt of knowing she had done something wrong, had experienced feelings and emotions she had had no right to feel... Had felt things... a need... a desire... A sense of excitement and pleasure it had been completely wrong for her to feel, and for a young man for whom she'd had no right to feel them. A young man who, in effect, had been a complete stranger to her. At sixteen she might have been naïve, physically innocent and unawakened, but she had known immediately just what her feelings were when she had felt those strong, youthful male hands touch her body.

She could still remember how it had felt to open her eyes, to be wrenched from the sensual bliss of a kiss which had literally made her untutored body tremble on the brink of orgasm, and then to hear the sound of her stepsister's malevolent voice.

'Look at her, Daddy... Look at her. She's nothing but a little whore... I did try to tell you.'

Shakily Courage abandoned her attempt to pick up the telephone receiver, her hands curling into two small protesting fists as she willed herself to ignore the torment of her memories, to push them away from her. It had been years now since she had last experienced anything like this, and she had actually begun to hope that she was finally beginning to get over what had happened.

She knew why this had happened, of course. It was Gideon Reynolds. Or rather it was her body's sexual reaction to his touch. She trembled under the shudder of self-revulsion she could not control.

It had never happened like this before—no real-life man had ever caused her to relive that hot, acid outpouring of guilt and shame combined with an equally searing, aching need.

'No.'

She said the word out loud, getting up and walking quickly over to the window. Hadn't she already got enough problems, enough things to worry about without adding this?

She had been sixteen... Naïve... Innocent... Never really intending to do anything wrong. But she *had* done wrong. Even though Gran had told her later, when she had finally coaxed her to unburden herself, that she was not really the one who was to blame.

Thank God for Gran. If she had not been there...had not realised that something was wrong...had not been concerned enough about her to persuade her mother to allow her to take her away... Courage shuddered again to think what fate might have ultimately befallen her if she had remained under her stepfather's roof.

But she was not under his roof any longer, she was under Gideon Reynolds', and she was supposed to be here to work. Determinedly she went back to the desk and reached again for the telephone.

She had already made herself known to all the other staff: the team of professional cleaners who came in daily to clean the house, the young mother who helped out in the kitchen, the gardeners and the men in charge of the golf course. From her conversations with them she had been able to build up a fairly clear picture of Gideon Reynolds' mode of life, although that, no doubt, would change slightly once his business activities were based full-time here rather than in London, as he apparently intended.

She had also discovered that his PA was not very popular with the rest of the staff, either the men or the women.

His presence among them was, she was pleased to learn, only a temporary one, since once Gideon had transferred his business to the house Chris would return permanently to London, where he would be in charge of the office Gideon wished to retain there.

With the exception of the PA, all the other staff appeared to think very highly of Gideon.

Courage prided herself on her professionalism where her work was concerned, and by the time Gideon returned she intended to have familiarised herself thoroughly with the demands of her new role.

After working in a series of busy five-star hotel complexes running one house, however large, should not present too many problems to her. But having to please a variety of guests who, no matter how demanding, would inevitably move on, was not like having to please one individual man who would not.

A swift check of Gideon's diary for the next month had shown her that in addition to the dinner party he had asked her to organise he would also be entertaining a small party of Japanese businessmen for four days, a group of officials from the Californian company who were consulting him about re-landscaping the large tracts of land devastated by fire, and a Kuwaiti prince and his entourage, as well as making several trips abroad himself.

This afternoon Courage planned to leave early, so that she could do some personal shopping before accompanying her grandmother on her first appointment with the heart specialist. They had both already been warned that before an operation could take place her grandmother would have to undergo a series of exploratory tests.

'All this fuss,' her grandmother had grumbled, 'and it's not even as though there is anything seriously wrong with me. I just get a bit tired and dizzy sometimes, that's all.'

'Think how much better you're going to feel afterwards,' Courage had coaxed her, trying not to let her own real feelings show.

In the morning, Courage was going to London to interview the woman who she hoped would take Alphonse's place, and then in the afternoon she and the woman in charge of the team of cleaners were going to go through the linen cupboards and allocate to each of the house's ten bedrooms its own specific supply of bedlinen and towels.

Gideon had employed a firm of interior designers to redecorate and refurbish the house and they had done an excellent job but, as the cleaning team had complained to her, there were simply not enough changes of bedding and towels.

'So far Mr Reynolds has only had a few guests staying here, but if the house was ever full...'

It was the same thing with the china cupboards. The interior designers had provided Gideon with an exquisite eighteenth-century dinner service, plus a good supply of basic, everyday crockery, but there were no individual breakfast sets, for instance, so guests could not be provided with breakfast in their bedrooms.

Since Gideon had given her *carte blanche* to purchase and order whatever she thought was necessary, Courage intended to take him at his word. There would be no point in telling him that his Japanese guests could not have breakfast in their rooms because they didn't have sufficient china and she had not wanted to buy any without his approval—she could already imagine just what his reaction would be.

Not that Courage intended to spend his money rashly or extravagantly. Even if her own nature had not done so, the training she had received from her thrifty Swiss employers would have ensured her good husbandry. She had already crossed two of her potential suppliers off her list, having crisply informed them that the discounts they were prepared to offer her were simply not good enough.

One of the first purchases she had made with money from the account Gideon had given her authority to open was a sturdy set of account books, into which she would meticulously list every expenditure as well as inputting the same details into the computer terminal which sat on a corner of the desk in the room she was using as her office.

She was just about to leave the office when her telephone rang. Putting down her jacket, she went to answer it.

The unexpected sound of Gideon's voice sent a sharp thrill of sensation shivering over her body. Swiftly she suppressed it, thankful that there was no one else in the room with her to see the betraying flush which had stained her skin.

'I wanted to speak to Chris but he isn't answering his phone,' Gideon told her. 'Is he there?'

'No. He did say that he would be spending this afternoon in London,' Courage informed him.

'I've tried the London office. He isn't there.'

Courage could hear the irritation in his voice. 'Is it anything I could help with?' she asked him, her training automatically coming to the fore.

'I doubt it... I seem to have omitted to bring with me a list of worldwide growers of the specialist plants we need for the Californian replanting scheme.'

Courage frowned, suddenly remembering how the cleaning team had complained about the state of Chris's desk and the general untidiness of the room he was using as an office. Courage had helped them to pick up some papers which had fallen off the desk in the draught from the open door. She was sure that one of them had been a list of specialist worldwide growers.

Quickly she explained the situation to Gideon, offering to ring him back when she had checked to see if the list was there.

'No, I'll hold,' he told her.

Three minutes later Courage was back on the line supplying him with the names he wanted but, rather to her chagrin, when he thanked her for her assistance instead of sounding pleased with her his voice seemed to hold a distinct note of curtness... of anger, almost.

Anger. The small thread of recognition which had tugged so elusively at her memory before suddenly became a thick cord of garotting strength, whipping tightly around her, paralysing her vocal cords, making her shake with shock, the cold sweat of fear springing from her pores.

No. It was impossible. It just couldn't be. She was imagining things. That voice—Gideon's voice—was not...

She was still clutching the receiver, even though the line had gone dead. She was completely alone in the empty room, with only the echo of Gideon's voice to remind her... Just as, all those years ago, she had also only been left with the echo of a bitterly angry and contemptuous male voice to remind her...

CHAPTER FOUR

COURAGE had been sixteen at the time, just sixteen, and very naïve and unworldly for her age.

Freshly home from boarding-school for the summer holiday, she had very quickly discovered in the few days she had been living under her stepfather's roof that nothing had changed; Laney was still out to make trouble for her, tormenting and persecuting her.

The older girl had come into her room late last night, laughing at her as she had started to flush with distaste and embarrassment when her stepsister had described to her, in intimate details, the evening she had just spent with her latest boyfriend.

'Not that any man's ever going to want someone as pathetic as you,' she added, tossing her head. 'I'll bet you haven't even been kissed properly yet, have you?'

Courage knew that her silence and her flushed face had given her away.

She might not have indulged in the kind of sexual intimacies Laney was so relishing describing to her, but that didn't mean that she did not have her own special daydreams, her private romantic fantasies about the man who would one day hold her in his arms and tell her that he loved her; the man whose very look would be enough to make her heart beat faster. She had already imagined how it would feel when he kissed her, the pleasure so exquisite that it almost made her faint with desire, but these imaginings and daydreams had nothing to do with the distasteful disclosures her stepsister was bragging about, and she knew far, far better than to reveal them to her.

'What are you blushing for?' Laney demanded now, her eyes narrowing maliciously as she accused her, 'I

know what it is—you've got a boyfriend, haven't you?
Who is he? Tell me...'

'Th-there isn't anyone,' Courage protested, stammering her denial painfully.

'Liar,' Laney taunted her. 'Just wait until I tell Dad.
He'll soon drag it out of you who he is...'

'No... No...you mustn't say anything to your father,'
Courage pleaded, her fear of her stepfather overwhelming the inner voice that warned her to be more
cautious.

'So there is someone. I knew there was.' Laney's eyes
were gleaming now, not with curiosity, Courage noticed,
but with triumph. There was a sick feeling in the pit of
her own stomach, an awareness that she had somehow
allowed herself to be trapped and that she was now at
her stepsister's mercy.

'All right, I won't say anything. But there's something
you've got to do for me...'

Tensely Courage waited.

'I've arranged to see this boy tomorrow night in the
summer-house, but now I can't go because I'm meeting
someone else. I want you to go instead, and tell him that
I can't make it.'

'Can't you get in touch with him? Telephone him or
something?' Courage suggested.

'Hardly. I don't suppose he even knows how to use a
telephone properly,' Laney told her contemptuously. 'He
works for the gardeners. I don't know why I agreed to
see him at all, really. I suppose I just felt sorry for him.
He's been pestering me for weeks. It's obvious that he's
totally besotted with me, but he's a fool if he thinks I'd
ever give someone like him a second glance. I
mean...he's a labourer, for God's sake... His hands
are filthy, his nails...' She gave a small dismissive shrug.

'So it's arranged, then,' Laney continued as she walked
towards Courage's bedroom door. 'You've got to be there
at nine o'clock, and just remember, Courage, if you're
not there, if you let me down, I'm going straight to
Daddy to tell him what you've been doing.'

'But I haven't been doing anything,' Courage protested, but she could see that it was too late. Laney was never going to believe her innocence now, and nor, she suspected, would Laney's father.

Her stepfather might be materially generous, but emotionally and physically he was extremely possessive. Courage had seen the rages he could fly into even with Laney when he thought she had been seeing someone of whom he disapproved, and she had heard him cross-questioning her own mother about who she had seen when she was out without him.

The last thing Courage wanted to do was to incur his wrath, to have him question her, even though in reality she had absolutely nothing to hide—no meetings of even the very most innocent kind with any boy to conceal from him.

'Just do as I've told you,' Laney warned her. 'Be at the summer-house for nine o'clock and tell him that I don't want to see him.'

'But it will be nearly dark by then,' Courage protested miserably. The summer-house was right at the bottom of their large garden, on the far edge of the lawn and surrounded by mature trees. There was no light down there and Courage felt apprehensive about going there to meet someone she didn't even know.

'Oh, dear, is the poor little diddums scared of the dark then? Oh, what a shame... It's your choice. Either you do as I've told you or I go to Daddy and tell him what you've been up to.'

Courage drew a shaky breath. 'All right,' she agreed helplessly, 'I'll do it.'

Courage shivered as she made her way down the dark path towards the summer-house. She was only wearing a thin, sleeveless cotton dress. Her stepfather had emerged from the bedroom he shared with her mother just as she had been on the point of going upstairs for her jacket, and rather than risk meeting him on the stairs she had come straight outside instead.

Since her return from school he had taken what was almost an oppressive interest in her; the criticisms which had preceded his announcement that she was to be sent away to school had been replaced by an even more uncomfortable over-solicitous concern, which made Courage reluctant to spend any more time than she needed to in his company.

Only the previous day he had announced that she was growing up and that it was time she had some new clothes. He would take her shopping, he had told her.

Courage had seen from the baleful look that Laney had given her how much she disliked this idea but had been unable to tell her stepsister that she disliked it just as much. Laney might be jealously possessive of her father's time and attention, but as far as Courage was concerned she was welcome to them.

She shivered again as the darkness of the garden enveloped her, but not purely from cold this time. She wasn't looking forward to having to tell Laney's date that her stepsister had changed her mind, but knew that Laney was more than capable of carrying out her threat if she refused to do so.

What did surprise Courage was that her stepsister had agreed to meet the boy in the first place. She normally never made any secret of the fact that in order to impress her a man had to be not just wealthy but well-connected as well.

Nervously Courage opened the summer-house door, tensing as it creaked slightly as she stepped inside. The small octagonal room smelt slightly musty. The building was very seldom used, although at one time, Courage suspected, it must have made a pretty venue for afternoon tea on a hot summer's day.

The silence and darkness was such that it was hard to remember that the relative safety of her stepfather's house was only a couple of hundred yards or so away.

As the seconds and then the minutes ticked away, without any sign of Laney's 'date', Courage began to hope that like her stepsister he had changed his mind.

But then, just as she was about to leave the summerhouse, she heard someone on the path outside; the door was pushed open and a tall, broad-shouldered male frame was blocking the doorway.

She couldn't see his face or distinguish his features— it was too dark for that—but she could smell the hot, male scent of him. Courage recognised that her own burgeoning sensuality and femininity were acutely aware of his maleness, of the sexual scent of him that was both far, far more subtle than any ordinary and more base body odour and yet, at the same time, so strongly, clamouringly intense that Courage automatically stepped back from him, out of range of its powerful spell.

'So you did come... I knew you would.'

His voice was slow and heavy, slightly slurred with something her shocked senses recognised as heavily aroused male desire.

'I knew you would, because, despite all those grand airs and graces you give yourself, you want me just as much as I want you...'

Courage could hear him breathing as he moved surefootedly towards her. Laney's excuse, the message she had been sent here to deliver was silenced, smothered even before she had time to think of uttering it as he crossed the distance between them, following her as she backed away in to the darkest corner of the summerhouse, his arms reaching for her, wrapping tightly around her, his body leaning into hers, imprisoning it against the wall as his head bent towards her.

'Now, let's see if you really can deliver all those things you've been promising me,' Courage heard him mutter thickly, his hand against her throat. The rough pad of his thumb stroked against her tender skin as he whispered things to her that shocked her into speechless silence at the same time as they sent a dizzying thrill of unfamiliar feelings zigzagging through her body in a jolt of electric sensation and as his mouth tormented her oversensitive skin with its biting kisses.

In the darkness, Courage tried to make out his features. His hair was dark, she could see that, and against the hands she had reached out in vain to hold him off she could feel the solid, powerful strength of his body.

His skin smelt clean and fresh, his breath slightly minty, and as she tried to turn her face away from him, panicking as she was hit by the realisation of what was happening, he cupped her face in one hand, preventing her doing so as he whispered rawly to her.

'What is it? Afraid that I might be too rough for that tender skin of yours? You needn't be... I've shaved...especially for you... Feel.'

And before Courage could stop him he had taken hold of her hand and pressed it against his jaw, gently dragging her fingertips up and down his skin.

In the darkness Courage could just see the flash of his eyes as he watched her, and saw as well as felt the way her whole body shuddered in uncontrollable reaction to what he had done.

Her heart was beating so fast it felt as though it was going to break through her chest-wall—and not from fear... Not any more.

She was breathing fast and very, very shallowly, and as his fingers circled her wrist and found the frantic pulse that raced there she could see the way his own chest lifted and fell in rapid counterpoint to her own dizzy excitement.

Courage had forgotten why she had come here; she was completely mesmerised by what was happening to her, totally oblivious to reality, awed and dazed by the discovery of her own sensuality and the power of the man holding her to arouse and excite it.

'I like you when you're like this, all shy and uncertain, like a virgin with her first man. But you're not a virgin, are you? No virgin looks at a man the way you've been looking at me.'

When Courage gasped, her eyes widening, he laughed softly.

'Oh, yes... Very good. You know all the tricks, don't you? All the ways to make a man feel good... to make him want you... But I want far more from you than pretended virginity. You know exactly what I want from you, don't you? And your body is telling me that you want the same things...' he growled against her mouth.

Courage tensed as he moved against her, grinding his hips into her so that she was shockingly aware of how hard his body was, how aroused.

'Oh, God. Come here and let me show you how much I want you...'

His voice was rougher now, his control slipping as his hands cupped her face and she felt his mouth move against her own, slowly at first, so that she could feel the full warmth of his lips. A thrill of wonder and pleasure twisted through her, her own mouth clinging with innocent seduction to his as she responded instinctively to his sensual exploration of her mouth.

No one had ever kissed her properly before, but somehow now that didn't seem to matter—her body, her senses seemed to know instinctively how she should respond.

'Hell, stop tormenting me. Open your mouth, kiss me back.'

The rawly agonised plea made Courage tremble. Her lips parted obediently, her heart thudding in frantic excitement as she felt the thrust of his tongue penetrating her mouth. His lower body was still moving against hers, its sensual movement and male hardness arousing all kinds of unfamiliar and shocking sensations deep inside her own body.

When his hand touched her breast she gave a small moan of shocked pleasure. Beneath her dress she could feel her nipples hardening. Her feelings were intensified by his low groan of reciprocal pleasure as he found the hard point of her breast and caressed it urgently with the pad of his thumb.

'I want you... God, how I want you.'

He was levering her away from the wall, reaching behind her for the zip of her dress, holding her so that her breasts...so that all of her was pressed tightly against him, as though he couldn't bear to break his contact with her, as though he couldn't bear to let her go.

Courage trembled wildly in his arms. This was just how she had imagined it would be—only more so. For she had never allowed her imaginings to take her this far...never truly realised just how wonderful it would feel to be kissed so passionately, to be told how much she was desired.

'You're trembling like a baby...'

She could hear the soft, male tenderness in his voice, and for some unknown reason it made her want to cling to him and cry.

'Don't worry... It won't be long now... Just let me get you out of this dress so that I can hold you close to me...feel your skin against mine. Touch and kiss you all over.'

As Courage shuddered, helplessly caught up in her own reaction to his words, she felt his breathing start to quicken.

'You want that, don't you? Well, I want it too. I'll just bet that you taste as sweet as honey and that you feel as soft and as expensive as pure silk. Oh, God, it's going to be so good for us... I want you so much...'

'I want you too...' Courage told him huskily, wrapping her arms around his neck, frantically kissing the exposed column of his throat, her fingers reaching out for the temptation of the dark body hair she could feel beneath his T-shirt as she waited for him to slide down the zipper of her dress.

Only suddenly he wasn't moving. Suddenly he wasn't holding her any more... Suddenly his hands were no longer caressing her but pulling away from her, placed on her shoulders as he thrust her almost roughly away from him, demanding furiously, 'What the hell is going on? You're not Laney—who the hell are you? Who the hell *are* you?'

The shock of his rejection, coming at the height of her own passionate desire for him, brought Courage abruptly back to reality, her whole body shivering in reaction as she realised what she was doing.

Sick shame engulfed her, her face burning with embarrassed heat. What on earth had come over her? Tears pricked her eyes, her throat closing up with pain and disbelief.

Now, with him standing half a dozen paces away from her, leaving her to stand alone in the cold damp of the evening air, it seemed impossible to believe that less than five minutes earlier they had been locked in a mutually passionate and intense embrace, wanting each other so desperately that...

Totally unable to comprehend what had happened, why she had behaved so...so recklessly, and in a way that was totally out of character for her, Courage could only stand there with shocked tears pouring silently down her face.

Why on earth had she let such a thing happen? Why hadn't she said something—told him that she wasn't Laney?

'What the hell's going on? Who the hell are you?' he repeated furiously. 'Come on, tell me.'

Courage flinched back into the deepest corner of the summer-house, frightened by his anger in a way that she had not been by his passion. Another wave of shame engulfed her as she remembered exactly how and what that had made her feel. A virgin she might be, but there were some things, some feelings, that even virgins could quite clearly interpret and understand.

'I'm...Courage Bingham. Laney is my stepsister,' Courage told him shakily, her voice low and taut with the intensity of her shame and fear. 'She...she asked me to meet you here so that——'

'So that what?' he interrupted her savagely. 'So that you could take her place? Why? It gives you some kind of kinky thrill, does it, comparing notes?'

'No... No...it wasn't like that,' Courage denied sickly. 'You don't understand, I——'

'Like hell, I don't,' he swore angrily. 'I understand all right... I understand that you were coming on to me like sweet hell, and that there was no way that hot, sexy little body of yours was going to stop giving out its "touch me, take me" signals to mine until it had got just what it wanted from me. And we both know what it wanted and how much, don't we?'

Courage made a soft, strangled gasp of protest deep in her throat, the tears rolling in silent swiftness down her face.

She wanted to cry out to him to stop it, to stop taking the delicate fabric of her dreams and tearing it, besmirching them, ripping them into tattered, grubby shreds.

When he had held her in his arms, kissed her, touched her, whispered his desire to her, she had felt the sweetest, purest surge of physical and emotional yearning. But now all that was gone, destroyed by his cruel condemnation of her. And yet, deep down inside, she felt that she deserved his cruelty. After all, it was not really *her* he had wanted, *her* he had believed he was holding and making love to, and he had every right to be furious with her for her unwitting deception of him.

'I didn't mean——' she began, trying to overcome her own emotions to explain to him that she had never intended to deceive him, but he wouldn't let her.

'You didn't mean what?' he challenged her bitingly, interrupting her. 'You didn't mean to go all the way? Well, I've got news for you, princess, the next time you play such a dangerous game you might not be so lucky. I happen to be a little bit choosy about who I bed— another man might not be. After all, when it's offered as blatantly as you were offering it to me——'

'Someone's coming,' Courage interrupted him, panic flaring inside her as she heard the male footsteps coming down the path. It could only be her stepfather... And instinctively she was afraid of what would happen if he found her here in the summer-house with this man.

'Quick, you must go. It will be my stepfather...' Without waiting for him to say anything, Courage darted past him and through the door. Her strongest instinct was not to protect herself but to protect him as she hurried towards the two people she could see coming down the path, praying that Laney's would-be lover, whoever he was, would be able to slip away without being seen.

'Look, there she is...I told you so,' Courage heard her stepsister cry out triumphantly as she hurried towards them.

'Courage, what are you doing down here...? Who have you been with?' her stepfather demanded furiously.

'No one...I haven't——' Courage started to lie unconvincingly, while Laney objected maliciously.

'She's lying, Daddy. I know who he is... What else would she be doing down here at this time of night other than meeting someone? Anyway, I heard her making the arrangements... I heard her on the telephone, telling him she would meet him here. The gardener's boy, of all people. Honestly... You'll have to sack him. You'd think she'd have more taste, but then again...perhaps not. Look at her, Daddy... Look at her. She's nothing but a little whore... I did try to tell you.'

Her stepfather had gone past Courage to inspect the summer-house, but to Courage's relief he found no one.

'Poor Courage—some lover,' Laney commented cruelly. 'I do hope you didn't let him go too far. Imagine letting someone like that paw you with his filthy hands...'

She gave a delicate fake shudder as her father came back to join them, swinging the torch he had been holding upwards so that Courage was caught mercilessly in its full beam.

'Oh, dear. He wasn't very gentle with you, was he?' Laney taunted her. 'He's left your mouth all bruised. But then that type goes in for that sort of thing...love-bites, I think they call them... Horrid, common bruises all over their lovers' necks... He hasn't left one on yours, has he...?'

Courage felt her skin start to burn as she remembered the delicately gentle and oh, so erotic sensation of his mouth sucking gently at her skin. Not on her neck, as Laney had suggested, but on the delicate inner flesh of her inner wrist and elbow.

The hours that followed were a nightmare of bitter accusations and recriminations, not just from her stepfather but from her mother as well. But through it all Courage steadfastly refused to betray her stepsister. What, after all, was the point? Who would believe her? And besides, she was guilty, wasn't she...?

She had allowed him, whoever he was, to kiss her, hold her, touch her... And in her own eyes, if not in those of her mother and stepfather, she had allowed him to make her feel the things so precious and sacred to her that she had promised herself only the man she loved would be able to make her feel; only the man she loved should cause that kind of emotional and physical response within her.

The shame of what had happened ate into her, causing her to keep to her room, unable to eat or sleep properly, and her shocked white face betrayed her feelings on the day her stepfather announced, in evident satisfaction, that he had arranged for her partner in crime to be dismissed from his job.

'No, you can't do that,' Courage had protested. 'It wasn't his fault.'

'See, Daddy, I told you,' Laney had pounced gleefully. 'She's admitting it. She's no better than she ought to be... I warned you what she was like...'

'Why... why did you do it...? Why did you bring your father down to the summer-house?' Courage asked her stepsister, when she finally got the opportunity to talk to her.

'Just a safeguard, that's all,' Laney told her lazily, grinning her triumph. 'He was the kind who wouldn't be easily put off. He took things more seriously than I intended. I realised that he'd probably keep on trying to pester me...make a nuisance of himself...start imagining that just because I'd been friendly towards him it meant something. Pathetic, really. I'm glad Daddy got him the sack.

'How far *did* he get, by the way, before he discovered you weren't me? Not very far, I'll bet. He must have found holding that cold, frigid body of yours a real turn-off. My God, I almost wish you *had* let him go all the way. Just imagine it, Little Miss Goody-two-shoes, pregnant by the gardener's labourer...'

She started to laugh, while Courage fought down the hot, bitter tears burning her eyes.

Two days later her grandmother arrived, and within the week, having seen how distressed and unhappy Courage was, she had persuaded her daughter-in-law, Courage's mother, to allow her to take formal charge of her grandchild.

If her stepfather hadn't been away on business at the time, Courage suspected she would not have been allowed to leave so easily, but for once the fates seemed disposed to be generous to her.

'Darling, I understand how you feel about this young man losing his job,' her grandmother told her gently, when Courage explained the situation to her, 'but we don't even know his name, or the name of the company he worked for, and you say Laney refuses to tell you, so I just don't see what we can do.'

Courage had been forced to accept that she was right, although why she should be concerned about the future of someone who had made it more than clear to her that he considered her a worse than poor substitute for her stepsister, she had no real idea.

CHAPTER FIVE

THE telephone rang, bringing Courage sharply back to reality and the present. She tensed for a moment, her body stiffening defensively as she reached out reluctantly to pick up the receiver. Her fingers trembled slightly as she curled them warily around it, but the voice on the other end of the line wasn't the one she was defending herself against hearing, it was her grandmother's.

'Courage, is everything all right?' she asked. 'Only, if you aren't going to be able to get back in time to drive me to the specialist's I can always get a taxi.'

It shook Courage to hear an unfamiliar note of uncertainty and frailty in her grandmother's voice. Guiltily she quickly reassured her.

'No, Gran, I'm just about to leave. Don't worry, we'll make it on time. I just got a little bit delayed.'

By the time she had driven home and collected her grandmother, Courage had managed to put her disturbing reaction to the sound of Gideon Reynolds' voice down to mere quixotic coincidence. It was, of course, impossible for Gideon Reynolds and that long-ago young man to be one and the same person, and heaven alone knew what peculiar subterranean workings of her psyche had been responsible for her ever imagining that they might be.

The telephone was notorious for distorting the sound of the human voice, and, besides, she had far more important matters to worry about than memories and emotions she ought to have pushed behind her years ago—such as her grandmother's health, for instance.

Quickly Courage glanced sideways to check on her grandmother. Was it her imagination, or did she really look a little frailer, a little bit older?

The situation wasn't critical yet—Dr Howard had said, adding, 'But with such a condition, nothing can ever be totally predicted . . . or taken for granted.'

Ruefully Courage discovered that she was pressing her foot down slightly harder on the accelerator, in an automatic reaction to her anxiety for her grandmother.

They were seeing the specialist in his private consulting-rooms in the city. Mentally Courage tried to calculate how long it would take them to park, and if they would be lucky enough to find a space close to the elegant row of eighteenth-century houses that ran alongside the river down from the ancient medieval wall which enclosed the original monastery hospice.

The city had a long medical connection, going back to the time of the monks who had established themselves in the area early in the eleventh century. After the Reformation, the Earl of Roewood, who had been rewarded for his support of the King, had been given the monastery and its surrounding lands. Aware of the ill-feeling the King's actions had caused in the area, he had gifted the monks' hospice to the city.

The original building had now been 'restored', along with what was left of the rest of the monastery, and provided a focal point for visiting tourists along with the cathedral and the cobbled medieval buildings and streets around it. A new hospital had now been built just outside the city, but many of the medical specialists who worked there kept to the old tradition of having consulting-rooms in the elegant row of houses.

Courage repressed a small sound of irritation as a coach cut across the road in front of her and then proceeded to block it as its driver tried to negotiate the sharp bend. In summer the city seethed with tourists, bringing into the area a good deal of very welcome extra income but at the same time impeding the progress of the normal everyday life of its citizens.

As they headed down towards the river Courage mentally kept her fingers crossed that they would find a parking space, otherwise she would have to drop her grandmother off outside the specialist's rooms and go and park the car somewhere else.

She suspected that, given the chance, her grandmother would try to persuade the specialist to minimise the severity of her condition. Not for her own sake but for hers, Courage acknowledged, breathing a small sound of satisfaction as she turned into the road which housed the specialist's rooms and saw a parking space almost immediately in front of them.

As she waited for her grandmother to get out of the car—she knew that if she attempted to help her, her grandmother would take it as another sign that Courage thought she was growing old and be angry with her for it—Courage admired the way the sunlight dappled the still slow-moving water of the river, shaded along its banks by the willows planted at the water's edge, behind which ran a carefully tended area of grass interspersed by wrought-iron and wooden benches.

A pair of swans and their signets sailed out from beneath one of the willows and out into the middle of the river, and Courage saw the sunlight bounce off cameras as tourists on a boat taking them down the river saw them as well and started to photograph them.

Sunshine warmed the red brick of the buildings as Courage and her grandmother crossed the road. A discreet black gold-lettered plaque outside one of them listed her grandmother's specialist as one of its occupants. Courage dutifully pressed the intercom buzzer and waited.

'So it's all agreed, then. I'll arrange for you to have the necessary tests and once we've got the results we can make a firm date for the operation.'

Courage suppressed a small sigh of relief as the specialist smiled at them both and started to stand up. There had been several moments during the consultation when she had feared that her grandmother was going to back out and refuse outright to go ahead.

Quickly she, too, got to her feet, determined to get her grandmother out of the consultant's chambers before she tried to change her mind.

But her grandmother had already forestalled her, saying firmly to the specialist, 'I still don't see why I can't wait and have the operation later. No, Courage,' she announced, before Courage could interrupt her, 'don't think I'm not grateful to you for what you want to do, but I still don't like the idea of you spending your money on me... On an operation I could have anyway if I just waited.'

'We've already been all through this, Gran,' Courage told her. Courage looked appealingly at the specialist. 'I've already explained to Gran that with hospital waiting-lists becoming increasingly long it might be that she has to wait *more* than another two years...'

Please don't let him say anything to her grandmother about how much more serious her condition was than she herself believed, Courage prayed inwardly as she watched him frown slightly as he looked from her anxious face to her grandmother's stubborn one.

'Your granddaughter is quite right,' he said calmly at last. 'Unpalatable though it is, it is an unfortunate fact of modern-day hospital and medical finances that funds can only be stretched so far, and, that being so, hospitals are now being forced to prioritise their operating-lists. Of course, we all realise that these days seventy is no age, and——'

'It's the full allocation of our biblical three score years and ten,' Courage's grandmother interrupted him. 'And to be honest with you...' She paused, her expression making Courage's heart suddenly start to thump heavily in foreboding.

Was it just the clear, cruel light of the strong summer sunshine that made her grandmother look so unfamiliarly tired, so vulnerable and shrunken somehow...? Of course, Courage hadn't been able to spend as much time with her as she would have liked over the last few years, just flying visits, in the main, when her grandmother had kept her so busy that she had barely had time just to sit and look at her.

'It's funny how your ideas change... When I was a young girl I wanted to live forever... But old age doesn't seem such a very appealing prospect once it's close at hand... I sometimes wonder if——'

'Gran——' Courage started to protest worriedly. But her grandmother shook her head and said firmly.

'Oh, it's all right, I'm not senile yet... It's just... sometimes... I feel so... so tired,' she admitted.

'Oh, Gran.' Courage's eyes filled with tears. She looked helplessly at the specialist, a tiny shiver of anxious fear running down her spine.

Her grandmother admitting to feeling tired... admitting that life... No, it was impossible... Her grandmother...

'All the more reason to have this operation as soon as possible,' Courage heard the specialist intervening firmly. 'I promise you that afterwards you'll look back on what you've said and laugh. You're tired because your heart's under such an awful lot of pressure,' he explained gently.

'It still seems such a waste of money,' Courage's grandmother protested, but there was less conviction in her voice this time, less determination as she looked from the specialist towards Courage.

'Of course it's not a waste,' Courage reassured her fiercely, swallowing back her tears as she took hold of her hand and told her thickly, 'Gran, you've done so much for me over the years, please let me do this one little thing for you... It would mean so much to me... *You* mean so much to me,' she added huskily. 'You're all I've got, Gran, and I don't want...'

She shook her head, unable to go on. 'I love you so much,' she told her grandmother.

On the other side of the desk the specialist cleared his throat emotionally.

'My secretary will write to you just as soon as a date had been arranged for tests... It will mean an overnight stay in hospital, of course.'

'It's all right, Gran,' Courage told her grandmother lovingly, squeezing her hand. 'Hospitals aren't like they used to be. It will be more like staying in a hotel these days.'

'And just as expensive,' her grandmother commented caustically, adding, with a return to her normal manner, 'And there's no need to tell me how much hospitals have changed, my girl. I think I'm in a rather better position to know that than you.'

'Yes, Gran,' Courage agreed meekly, too thankful to see her rallying round to take her to task for her comment.

One of the many ways in which her grandmother gave time to her local community was via a hospital-visiting scheme for those patients who had no one close of their own to visit them.

'I'm not in my dotage yet, you know,' she added severely.

'No, Gran,' Courage agreed meekly.

'Well, I'm ready for bed even if you aren't,' Courage informed her grandmother the next evening. She wanted to be at work early in the morning. The new cook was due to arrive at ten and Courage wanted to have her desk cleared of the morning's post and all her other routine chores finished before she arrived so that she could show her the kitchens and go through everything with her.

'Courage, as grateful as I am, I do still feel your money should be saved for when you have a family,' her grandmother said quietly. 'When I was your age, I'd been married for two years and had had your father...'

'Things were different then, Gran,' Courage told her gently. 'These days our sex has far more options open to it... You were the one who encouraged me to think in terms of a career...who told me how important it was for me to be able to be independent...'

'And so it is,' her grandmother confirmed stoutly. 'But I still can't help thinking... That business all those years ago with your stepfather and that daughter of his... It didn't...'

'My decision to concentrate on my career has nothing to do with them,' Courage denied, not entirely truthfully. 'Perhaps I haven't met the right man yet, Gran...' Or perhaps she had met him and been rejected by him, a tiny inner voice taunted her.

At sixteen? She had been far too young...too immature...too inexperienced to know the first thing about love—the kind of love needed to build a strong, secure marriage, the kind of marriage she wanted. And he had been a stranger. And if the mixture of guilt and anxiety she felt whenever any man approached her sexually really was based on some deeply concealed psychological reaction to what had happened with him, and not, as she had always preferred to tell herself, an unfashionable lack of strong sexual desire, then...

Then, what?

She was being ridiculous, she told herself sternly. Just because for some odd reason hearing Gideon Reynolds' voice yesterday afternoon had reminded her of the past, of him, that was no reason for her to feel she had to go burrowing around in the depths of her subconscious. Hadn't she got enough to worry about with Gran, without that kind of silly emotional self-indulgence?

It was probably the shock of Gran's ill-health that was bringing all these old memories to the surface, she told herself comfortingly. And now that Gran had seen the specialist, and agreed to allow her to pay for her treatment, no doubt she should soon be back to normal, the ghosts of her past firmly sent back to where they belonged.

It was just gone six o'clock in the morning when Courage arrived at work on Wednesday. Her grandmother had shaken her head in disbelief last night when Courage had told her what time she planned to be at work, but Courage had laughed.

'In the hotel trade you get used to working all kinds of different shifts,' she had told her. 'And to working right through on a double shift sometimes, if it becomes necessary.'

'If you're not careful *you'll* be the one who needs to go into hospital, not me,' her grandmother had warned her darkly.

It looked as if it was going to be another fine day, Courage decided as she glanced at the clear blue sky. There was no warmth in the sun as yet and the lawns were heavy with dew, calm and untouched, like the day itself. Courage loved this time of the morning; it was one of her favourite times of the day. Humming to herself, she let herself into the house and headed straight for her office.

Half an hour later she was deeply immersed in her work, her fingers flying over the keyboard as she prepared a new worksheet for the cleaning staff. Although she could not fault their work, she suspected that their current routine could be reorganised to be more efficient.

She frowned as she stopped typing for a moment. What exactly did Gideon Reynolds have in mind for this dinner party he was planning for tomorrow? And he hadn't informed her yet how many people he would be bringing back with him when he returned from his trip, or what his plans for them were. Because he wanted to test her?

She had already arranged for three of the guest suites to be made ready. Would that be enough? Her stomach rumbled protestingly as she pondered the matter, reminding her that she had left home without breakfast.

She glanced at her watch. Almost seven. She might as well grab the opportunity to make herself a coffee and have a piece of toast while she could. As she poured cold water into the filter coffee-machine Courage acknowledged that the kitchen was well-planned, even if Alfonso had complained, his lip curled in disgust, that it was a 'cook's kitchen' not a chef's. In other words, a woman's and not a man's.

Well, she hoped the new cook she had engaged to take his place agreed with him, Courage decided as she heated up some milk in the microwave and removed her toast from the toaster.

She had just taken her first bite of it, still standing up, when the kitchen door was unexpectedly thrust open and Gideon Reynolds strode in demanding angrily, 'What the hell are you doing here, and where's Alfonso?'

Courage stared at him in shocked confusion, her toast forgotten.

'You weren't supposed to be coming back until later today,' she heard herself saying weakly. She could feel the fine skin of her face burning with hot colour—not just because of his unexpected appearance, not even because of the way he had spoken to her, like a child caught out in some misdemeanour. No, the reason for her heightened colour had a far more direct cause than that.

Did he make a habit of striding around the house like that, his body very plainly completely nude apart from the thin, *very* thin silk boxer shorts he was wearing?

Courage had seen equally nude men before, plenty of them, but for some reason, she couldn't take her gaze off this one. It remained disobediently riveted to the muscled male torso of the man now standing less than a couple of metres away from her, his eyebrows snapping together in an irritable frown as he waited for her to respond to his question.

Courage knew she ought to look away... She *wanted* to look away. There was no way that those silk shorts came anywhere near remotely concealing the extremely male anatomy of her new employer. Covering it, yes. Concealing it—no.

Gripped by a paralysing fascinated and shocked awe, Courage knew that it wasn't just her face, but her whole body now that was covered in that betraying give-away scarlet flood of female awareness of him. Was that line of silky dark hair that disappeared beneath the waistband of his shorts, really as temptingly soft to touch as it looked? Was it...?

Courage could hear someone breathing with shaky heaviness. Embarrassed, she realised it was herself. She was trembling as well, she recognised, and her heart was beating far too fast.

All because of Gideon Reynolds?

Quickly she wrenched her gaze away from his body. She felt as cold now as she had felt hot before, her teeth threatening to start chattering. She must be in some kind of shock, she told herself, and no wonder... He was the *last* person she had expected to see... Especially dressed, or rather undressed like that...

'Is something wrong?'

The earlier irritation had left his voice now and it was suddenly as smooth as cream, the look in his eyes as she glanced briefly towards him alerting her to the dangerous situation her foolishness had created...

Did he think, perhaps, that she had been giving him a come-on? she wondered uncomfortably. If so, she must correct that impression. Couldn't he tell, the difference between shock and desire? she wondered crossly. What woman *wouldn't* stare at a man who strode totally unexpectedly into a kitchen dressed only in...in what *he* was wearing... Especially when that man was her employer and she...

This *was* his home, she reminded herself.

'You gave me a shock,' she told him, lifting her head and forcing herself to meet the look in his eyes head-on. 'You said you'd be returning late this evening...'

'So I changed my mind.' He gave a careless shrug, adding with a frown, 'What are you doing here anyway? It isn't nine o'clock yet.'

'I...I wanted to get here early. To...' She paused, suddenly flustered by the way he was watching her. 'I really think you ought to get dressed before we continue this discussion,' she told him primly.

'Do you? You do surprise me,' he responded softly. 'From the look you were giving me five minutes ago I'd have said that what you *really* wanted was the exact opposite to that statement... What's wrong?' he taunted her, as Courage flushed in mortification. 'And don't even bother trying to tell me that you've never seen a man dressed like this before...

'Not that your reaction wasn't flattering,' he continued, ignoring her small gasped protest. 'Flattering, but really rather overdone. I know that all men are supposedly over-vulnerable to their egos where their male attributes are concerned... But since I'm quite well aware that mine are...relatively modestly average, you're rather wasting your time. And in any case, isn't it supposed to be what you do with it that's really important, not what size it is...?'

Courage didn't know what to say or do. No man, especially not one whom she hardly knew, had ever spoken like this to her before, and her flush deepened as Gideon continued smoothly.

'From the way you were looking at me anyone would think you'd never seen a man's body before, and we both know that that's very far from the truth. Now, I repeat, where is Alfonso? I've got a busy day scheduled and I want my breakfast.'

The speed with which he changed from taunting sexual male to boss caught Courage off-guard. She stared at him in confused silence for several seconds before managing to stammer, 'Alfonso. Well, actually, he's...he's gone...'

'Gone? Gone where, and why?'

Haltingly Courage explained, her gaze firmly focused on a spot just to one side of him as she acknowledged the danger of allowing it to stray anywhere near his body.

'I have taken on a new cook...subject to your approval, of course. She'll be arriving this morning... At ten...'

'Ten.' He gave her a grimly derisory look as he glanced at the kitchen clock.

Courage followed his gaze. It was just gone seven-thirty.

'I've got a meeting with my accountants in the city at nine-thirty,' he told her. 'What would you have done if you'd found yourself in this situation in your previous post: a hotel full of guests who needed feeding and no chef?'

'That would never have happened. I'd have cooked for them myself, if necessary,' Courage informed him quickly.

Too late, she saw the trap he had so neatly sprung on her as she watched the mocking smile curl his mouth.

'I'll have fruit juice, coffee, toast—wholemeal bread— oh, and some fruit muesli with natural yoghurt. Bring it up to my room as soon as it's ready, will you? You do know where my room is, don't you?'

Oh, yes, she knew where his room was. But if he thought she was going to make his breakfast for him...

Indignantly she opened her mouth, and then closed it again as her normal cautious good sense overtook her sense of outraged female pride.

What he was asking for was, in fact, no less—although certainly rather less politely put—than requests she had had in the past from her employers to help out by taking on tasks in an emergency which were, strictly speaking, outside her remit.

It had never even occurred to her to refuse them...

But it had never been something so personal as making their breakfast that they had asked for, and neither had they ever made her feel as Gideon Reynolds was doing— that they enjoyed using their authority over her to compel her to perform a more personal task than she would normally have been expected to do.

But if she refused, and he dismissed her, how on earth was she going to pay for Gran's operation?

All the doubts and forebodings she had felt when she had originally taken the job now returned. Accepting Gideon Reynolds' offer of a loan had trapped her, taking the control of her professional life out of her own hands.

If Gideon Reynolds commanded that she get down on her hands and knees and scrub his floors, there would be very little she could do about it.

Swallowing her anger, she turned away from him, asking as calmly as she could, 'How do you prefer your coffee?'

'Black, filter and plenty of it,' came the cool response. 'And for future reference, I prefer my muesli to be home-made...'

'I'll pass that information on to the cook,' Courage told him stonily. 'Shall I defer taking her on until you have had a chance to interview her yourself, by the way?'

'When I hired you it was in the belief that you had both the experience and the confidence to take full responsibility for all the domestic details of running this place. If you really need to have every small decision you make backed up by me then you're the wrong person for the job...'

Mortified, and furious with herself for giving him the opportunity to criticise her, Courage compressed her mouth. 'Chris seemed to think you would prefer to have a male chef rather than a female cook. A chef is, of course, more of a status symbol...'

'And I am the kind of man who needs to surround himself with status symbols... Is that what you're trying to imply?'

The cool voice had a distinctly hostile edge to it now, and Courage shivered nervously inside her skin.

'I...I wasn't trying to imply anything,' she back-pedalled, refusing to let him completely overwhelm her as she added more firmly, 'It's a fact of life that we live in a world where outward appearances can be important and in which we are often judged on the image we present to the world. Your business obviously involves creating the right kind of impression to win clients and contracts...'

The dark eyebrows snapped together frowningly.

'I hardly think that if my knowledge and ability in my field was faulty employing a chef as opposed to a cook would do much to mend matters.'

'No,' Courage agreed, 'but, as they say, success breeds success, and the creation of an outer image that says you are successful is bound to have a psychologically reassuring effect on prospective clients.'

'Oh, indeed, self-confidence and self-assurance are reassuring—just as long as they're backed up by something a good deal more substantial, like ability... for instance,' he told her smoothly. 'I certainly found your references and your past experience extremely reassuring as a prospective employer. However, right now I'm beginning to wonder just how reliable they actually are.

'So far, you've been in my employ less than a week. My chef has left and I return home to find there's no one to take his place. What would have happened, for instance, if I'd brought some prospective clients back with me?'

What would have happened? He had a point, Courage acknowledged.

'If that had been the case I'd have had to prepare their breakfast myself,' she told him quietly, and then blushed. How could she explain to him when she couldn't even explain to herself that there was something about the intimacy of preparing breakfast just for him rather than doing so for a group of people that had set in action some deep-rooted female wariness?

She couldn't. Instead, she said stiffly, 'I'll bring your breakfast up just as soon as I can...'

Somehow she just managed to resist the temptation to add the word 'sir' to her sentence, sensing that his retaliation, should she do so, would be swift and devastating.

As soon as he had left the kitchen Courage went quickly to check the fridge, her heart sinking as she confirmed what she had already known. She had deliberately refrained from stocking up with any food, preferring to wait until the new cook had arrived so that she would be free to choose her own supplies.

It was not yet eight o'clock in the morning, and the nearest supermarket was in the city—too far away, an all-round trip of at least three-quarters of an hour. And then she remembered seeing a new service station that had recently opened. Keeping her fingers crossed that it was one of those which had its own small shop, she snatched up her bag and hurried out to her car.

Fifteen minutes later she was back, triumphantly unpacking her purchases. Oranges—she already knew the kitchen was supplied with a juicer—natural yoghurt, wholemeal bread and muesli. Quickly she found the juicer and cut the oranges before going to make some fresh coffee.

Refusing to allow herself to be panicked, she worked swiftly and efficiently, trying to imagine she was back in Switzerland in her first job, obediently watching the chefs working in the kitchen. Ten minutes later she had prepared the breakfast tray.

Unclipping her hair, which she had fastened back while she worked with the food, she smoothed it down with her hands and then, taking a deep breath, picked up the tray, walking determinedly towards the stairs. She had only been inside Gideon's suite of rooms once before, on her original exploration of the house; it comprised a large, surprisingly comfortably furnished sitting-room-cum-study, an even larger bedroom, a dressing-room and a bathroom.

In addition to buying the food at the service station, Courage had also purchased several newspapers, plus a copy of the *Economist* when she had noticed that the current issue was running an article on the increasing problem of over-cultivation of once semi-fertile farmlands in desert areas. No doubt it wouldn't contain anything that Gideon didn't already know, but even so...

In fact, she would be rather interested to read the article herself. Although she was semi-loath to admit it,

Gideon's work had captured her imagination, and she was keen to learn more about it.

To her relief, the sitting-room was empty when she went in. She was just about to put the tray down on the desk when she heard Gideon call out to her from the bedroom.

'Bring it here will you, please, Courage?'

Hesitantly she turned towards the half-open bedroom door, her footsteps slowing slightly, reflecting her reluctance to walk into the bedroom. Reminding herself that she had on countless numbers of occasions had to walk into hotel bedrooms occupied by men, and had had to deal with male guests in various stages of undress, she took a deep, calming breath and stepped through the communicating doorway. The realisation that Gideon wasn't actually in the bedroom made her frown and check it a second time.

'Thanks. Just leave it over there by the window, will you?'

The sound of Gideon's voice coming from behind her made her whirl round just in time to see him emerging from the bathroom.

The dark silk shorts had been replaced by a soft white towel draped round his hips. His body and hair were both still damp from his shower and as he came towards her Courage could smell the clean, sharp scent of his soap.

Instinctively she took a step backwards, her hands tightening defensively around the tray as she tried to avoid looking at the small beads of water running down over his skin. Her unwanted awareness of him made her slow and clumsy, and she gasped out loud as Gideon reached out, halting her backward progress by placing one hand on the tray she was holding. The other he raised to push the damp hair back off his forehead.

Shockingly Courage felt her own skin start to bead uncomfortably with moist heat, a swift, sharp sensation she was too horrified to name zigzagging through her body as she watched almost mesmerised as the muscles in his raised arm flexed and she saw the dark silky dampness of his underarm hair.

Why was it that the sight of body hair on this man should be so urgently and erotically arousing for her, when normally...? She was beginning to feel slightly faint and dizzy, her heart racing furiously.

'Where did you get this?' she heard Gideon asking her frowningly, as he removed the copy of the *Economist* from the tray.

'I...I bought it at the garage. I had to go there for...for some food...' Courage explained huskily. 'I...I thought you might find the article interesting.'

She flushed as brilliantly as a teenager as she felt him looking at her. What was the matter with her? She'd made herself sound as though his approval was important to her... as though... as though...

'Mm... Yes... I expect they'll send me a complimentary copy. It's several months since I wrote the article for them, now... but of course nothing has really changed—except perhaps for the worse.'

It took several seconds for the meaning of his words to sink in fully, but once they had Courage felt herself flushing even more deeply than she had done before. *He* had written the article. Why on earth hadn't she looked a bit closer at the magazine? Now he was either going to think she was slapdash in not having realised that he was the author of the article or sycophantic in having noticed and then having bought the magazine as a way of flattering him and getting into his good books.

Of the two alternatives, she would infinitely prefer him to choose the former, Courage acknowledged grimly. And, since honesty was an ethic she firmly believed in practising, she took a deep breath and, hoping that the tell-tale colour flushing her skin wouldn't betray her any further, owned up quickly, like someone swallowing a nasty dose of medicine.

'I'm sorry. I bought the magazine on impulse, without realising that you had written the article.'

Inwardly she was cursing herself. Of course she should have realised that at the very least he would have been consulted over such a subject, since he was an acknowledged worldwide expert in the field.

What was it about this man that constantly put her on the defensive? Made her feel so wary...so almost insecure about herself and her skills? Made her feel as though he were in some way setting traps for her, testing her, wanting her to fail? She frowned to herself. Now she *was* being silly. He had, after all, chosen her to work for him.

She was still uncomfortably conscious of his near-nude state, and had deliberately kept her glance fixed very firmly away from his body. The tension her awareness of him was creating inside her made her long to escape, but a certain streak of stubborn pride refused to allow her to give in to such a vulnerable feminine desire.

Instead she gritted her teeth and reminded him, 'Before you left you mentioned a dinner party that you intended to hold.'

'Yes,' he agreed, his frown deepening, his voice suddenly unexpectedly terse—so terse, in fact, that Courage was betrayed into looking at him.

Fortunately he had turned his head aside slightly, but she could still see the strong, decisive groove that ran alongside his mouth and the compressed hardness of his jaw.

'I had intended to invite several of my neighbours to dine tomorrow, but it seems that the majority of them are unable to, so Chris informs me.'

Now it was Courage's turn to frown. She was no fool. In the course of her working life she had come across people from very many different walks of life and she was well aware of the sense of ill-usage and inferiority that many people who had made their own way in the world felt towards those who, in their worldly terms, were considered 'better born', for want of a different expression.

At the hands of her hotel guests Courage had herself experienced the most appallingly rude behaviour and the most heart-warmingly friendly and polite—across a very broad spectrum of social classes. She had met self-made millionaires whose manners and attitudes had made her heart lift in warmth, and high-born aristocrats whose attitudes had filled her with the utmost pity and con-tempt—and the reverse was equally true.

That being the case, she found it hard to understand why an apparently large proportion of Gideon's neigh-bours should refuse his invitation. Unless there was some specific way in which he had offended them.

One or two refusals could be expected, and would probably be quite genuine, but more than that... The days were surely gone when a man was excluded from 'society' because he was not considered to be of the 'right' class and background?

'It *is* summer,' she responded carefully. 'I expect that people will be going away...'

'Very tactful,' Gideon complimented her acidly. 'But a bit pointless in the circumstances, don't you think? According to Chris—— Where is he, by the way?' he asked her. 'I expected him to be here.'

'He hasn't returned from London yet,' Courage told him. She was still curious about why so many of Gideon's neighbours should have refused his dinner invitation, but she knew she would not gain any more out of Gideon himself and suspected that he was already regretting what he had said to her.

There were other sources of information, though. Not that her interest was motivated by any kind of prurient curiosity, she assured herself quickly. It was just that if there was any specific reason for his neighbours' refusal to have anything to do with Gideon she ought to know about it—for her own protection, if nothing else.

'Perhaps if you were to suggest an alternative date for your dinner party?' she suggested.

Gideon gave her a withering look before pushing his hand through still damp hair, an action which caused his towel to move fractionally lower on his hips and Courage's stomach to do spectacularly blood pressure-raising cartwheels. Quickly she looked away from him, uncomfortably aware of the fine film of sweat dampening the sensitive flesh just above her upper lip and the valley between her breasts.

Like an animal seeking cover...camouflage...she started to head for the bedroom door.

'Where are you going?'

Her spine stiffened rebelliously at the imperious tone of Gideon's voice, but cravenly she found herself stopping and half turning round to face him in response to its command.

'I... I... You...'

She watched warily as he picked up the glass of fruit juice and tasted it.

'Fresh fruit...good,' he told her. 'What time did you say you were seeing Alfonso's replacement?'

'She's arriving about ten,' Courage responded. 'She's quite happy to live in and she's worked in catering for almost twenty years—both small and large businesses. Her qualifications are excellent and I felt she had the right type of personality for this kind of work—she's very calm and used to working to a tight schedule when necessary. However, if you feel...'

'No, I trust your judgement—professionally.'

Courage frowned. Was it her imagination or had there been a slight emphasis on the word 'professionally'? And if so, why?

'After all, that's what I'm paying you for—and very well,' Gideon added coolly. 'However, before you go, there is something...'

For no reason that she could explain, Courage felt her stomach starting to sink. Uneasily she watched as Gideon crossed the room and disappeared into his dressing-room. What was he doing? she wondered edgily... Making her wait while he got dressed? She only wished he would put some clothes on. The sight of his near-naked body had disturbed her in more ways than she wanted to admit...

It hadn't just been mere feminine embarrassment that had brought the hot blood rushing up under her skin, although she hoped that only she was aware of that.

She stiffened as she realised that Gideon was coming back. Her body tensed as she saw that he was still only wearing a towel—a dry one by the looks of it—that was hitched slightly higher and rather more firmly around his hips than the original had been. He was, she observed, carrying a small box. Her tension increased as he beckoned her towards him. Reluctantly she crossed the small expanse of carpet which separated them.

'Take it,' Gideon ordered her when she was standing close enough for him to hold out the small box to her.

'What...what is it?' she asked him nervously. Her heart was pounding far too fast and she was conscious of that unfamiliar and dangerous heat invading her body again.

'Open it and see,' Gideon told her.

Gingerly Courage did as he instructed, surprise replacing her wariness as she opened the box and saw nestling inside it a heartbreakingly delicate fine gold chain.

'It's to replace the one that broke,' Gideon told her briefly.

Courage was still staring at the contents of the box. Even without lifting it from its nest of protective tissue, Courage knew that the chain was of far better quality and far more expensive than her own. The gold alone was obviously far purer, and the workmanship of the fine coils of gold so intricate that she was loath even to touch it. She doubted that her own chain would have cost one tenth as much as this one. Blankly she raised her eyes to meet Gideon's hard, impatient stare.

'I can't accept this,' she told him.

For a moment he looked almost nonplussed, as though she had somehow shocked him.

'It's far too expensive...far too valuable,' she told him, taking advantage of his silence. 'I...'

'You, what...?' Gideon asked her softly, back in control once again. 'You only accept that kind of gift from a lover? You have the kind of skin that suits gold,' he added, shocking her into silence. 'Gold and pearls. There's something very erotic about dressing a naked woman with jewels. No wonder the Arabian potentates used to command that their concubines wore nothing else.'

'That's disgusting,' Courage told him furiously. 'It's... it's both sexist and demeaning. Why don't you go the whole way and say that women should be tied up in chains, imprisoned in them, turned into helpless captives... sex-slaves?'

Courage knew she was overreacting, but something in his words had reactivated a long-buried memory of her stepfather giving her a birthday gift—a small, delicate gold bracelet. Laney had been there when he gave it to her, a watchful, taunting expression in her eyes. Very reluctantly Courage had accepted the gift, immediately going to place it on her wrist, until Laney had laughed mockingly at her.

'Not there, stupid, it goes round your ankle...like mine.' As she spoke she had displayed a small tanned ankle, waving it around so that the gold chain adorning it glinted.

Without understanding why, Courage had immediately felt uneasy and apprehensive. She had stepped back from her stepfather as he reached out to place the anklet on, shaking her head in rejection. He had been furious with her, of course, and her mother had been upset. Courage had been sent to her room without any supper and the incident pushed to the back of her mind—a mind too young and immature to have been able to deal with a situation it had found both frightening and humiliating with its undertones of sexuality and bondage.

Now that long-buried memory had resurfaced, bringing with it all the emotions she had not been able to express. Automatically, as she spoke, she stepped back from Gideon, her whole body quivering with anger and outrage, the shadow of those old memories darkening her eyes so that she looked both magnificently furious and femininely vulnerable.

At the same time the anger she was expressing as she stepped back from him was totally adult, an all woman fury at what he had said, while the look in her eyes and the betrayingly expressive cowering rejection of her body were the body language of a frightened child.

'Courage——' he began impulsively.

But she was holding up her hand in denial, shaking her head as she told him unsteadily. 'No... don't. No, I don't want to hear any more.'

Placing the small box down on the edge of the bed, Courage turned and fled.

Once she was back in the security of the kitchen, she began to regret what she had done and what she might have betrayed. It had been stupid of her to allow herself to be drawn into such a dangerously intimate exchange and oddly, despite the way he had taunted her, she had a very deep-rooted feeling that Gideon Reynolds was not the kind of man who liked his women sexually passive, or one who needed the sexual stimulation of playing fetishistic bondage games.

Which meant that he had deliberately tried to bait her. But why?

She was still pondering the question a little later on, when she heard him come downstairs. She tensed as she heard his footsteps coming towards her office, glad to have the protective bulk of her desk between them when he came in.

He was fully dressed now, in a crisp white shirt and a dark business suit which gave him an imposing air of authority.

'If Chris appears will you tell him that I want to see him?' he asked Courage, his manner as formal and businesslike as his appearance. No trace of his earlier very male sexuality was in evidence.

As he turned away from her and walked back through the still open kitchen door Courage drew in a short, shaky breath, which she was still holding several seconds later and went on holding until she heard him open and close the front door.

Well, this morning had convinced her of one thing, at least: that trick of the telephone wires which had made his voice sound so shockingly similar, familiar, had been nothing more than that... a trick.

Listening to him this morning... watching him... she had felt no similar sense of recognition at all. The clean, sharp smell of his body had been nothing like the aroused musky scent she remembered. A tiny shudder convulsed her body, her face burning hot with remembered discomfort.

The only thing the two men did have in common was that both of them—— She stopped, unwilling to continue with her uncomfortable and unwanted train of thought.

That sharp pang of sexual hunger she had felt so recently had been nothing other than an odd fluke... A... physical aberration... Just because the only other time she had ever felt anything similar to it had been in a dark London garden, held tight in the arms of an unknown man, didn't mean... Didn't mean anything, she told herself fiercely.

The last, the very last complication she needed in her life right now was to start feeling... To start *wanting* Gideon Reynolds. The very last!

'This is a lovely area. I can't wait to start work here.'

Courage smiled at the other woman's open enthusiasm. Her interview with Jenny Carter had confirmed her original opinion of her. Her qualifications were excellent and, unlike Alfonso, she showed no signs of a difficult or volatile temperament.

'I've been wanting to get away from city living for some time,' she confessed to Courage. 'I was brought up in the country and I miss it. Now that both my children are grown up and settled into their own lives it's much easier to take the decision to make a change of lifestyle.'

The interview over, they were walking across the gravel to where Jenny's car was parked. Courage knew that Jenny's husband, who had been over a decade older than her, had died two years earlier and that she was now alone.

'You must miss him,' she had said sympathetically when Jenny told her.

'Yes, I do,' she had agreed. 'But at least I have my family and friends and my work, although of course it is never quite the same.'

She had raised her eyebrows when, in answer to one of her questions, Courage had told her that Gideon wasn't married.

'Mmm... Why not I wonder? A man of his age and with his wealth. He can't have been short of opportunities.'

'His work takes him all over the world,' Courage had explained, brutally stifling the small, sharp ache her words had caused. Why should she care whether or not Gideon was married? She didn't. She *couldn't*, she told herself fiercely.

'Mmm... Well, a lot of men of his type do tend to marry late, and then to some pretty young thing who they believe they can mould into a cross between a child and an obedient slave. Not that it normally works. Inevitably their pretty, wide-eyed girl-brides grow up and want to be treated as women—as adults. I've seen it happen so many times. Still, I don't suppose it's really any of our business,' she had added briskly.

Changing the subject slightly, she had gone on, 'You did mention at our original interview that there would be occasions when there could be a substantial amount of business and social entertaining?'

'Potentially, yes,' Courage had agreed, choosing her words carefully, remembering what Gideon had said about his neighbours refusing his invitation. 'But that's something we can discuss once you've settled in.'

They had agreed that Jenny was to move over the weekend and settle herself in, and that she and Courage would go through the store cupboards and organise themselves properly early the following week.

Jenny would be taking over the small self-contained flat which had been Alfonso's—one of several staff flats built over the garage and stable-block.

The two of them would work well together, Courage knew, provided Gideon approved of her decision to employ Jenny. They had agreed on a month's trial on either side.

'Not that I expect to change my mind,' Jenny informed Courage before she drove off.

'Me, neither,' Courage assured her. 'But, of course, the final decision doesn't rest with me.'

CHAPTER SIX

COURAGE frowned, focusing her concentration on the computer screen in front of her as she studied the figures she was checking—household accounts for the period before Gideon had employed her.

They should have been straightforward enough, and initially the only reason that Courage had been studying them had been to see what kind of monthly expenditure the upkeep of the property necessitated. She had already drawn up her own prospective budgets, but before she presented them to Gideon she wanted to make sure that they were not too far out of line with what was normally spent.

Rather disconcertingly, though, she had discovered that her budget forecasts were considerably lower than the expenses for the previous periods—and not in any one specific area. The extra expense was spread over almost the whole of the household budget.

Having always worked in the hotel trade, where keeping overheads down meant the difference between making a profit and going bankrupt, she had initially been puzzled by so much unnecessary wastage. However, a closer look at the accounts had brought to light something rather more serious.

Was she leaping to unwarranted conclusions? Or were her suspicions that Chris Elliott had deliberately padded out the household expenses correct?

Her head was aching slightly, and not merely because of the long period of time she had spent staring at the computer screen. Her grandmother was going into hospital today for her tests. Courage very much wanted to go with her, but Gideon was due back from a business trip to Kuwait.

He had flown out there almost immediately after his return from America, and Courage felt apprehensively on edge at the thought of his return.

It had shocked her to discover that the reason he had been so anxious to see his PA before he left had been because he wanted to sack him—now she suspected she knew the reason why.

Courage had heard their raised voices from her own office; or at least one voice had been raised. Some of the comments she had heard Chris making about his own upper class family background and upbringing in comparison to—according to *his* judgement—Gideon's much more lowly social status, had filled her with both shock and contempt.

Although Gran rarely mentioned it, her grandparents had been titled but impoverished Scottish landowners. Gran's mother—their daughter—had married a second son with no title, and Gran herself, of course, had then been a mere 'Miss', as opposed to her cousin's more socially elevated 'Honourable' and 'Lord Robert...'

The families still kept in touch—over the years Courage had attended her share of very grand weddings and christenings—but she felt neither envy of her distant titled relatives nor the slightest desire to boast of her connections with them.

Why should she? She was perfectly content with the person she was and with her own role in life.

She had always scorned and loathed the kind of attitude she had heard Chris loudly expressing. To Courage his comments were both ugly and self-demeaning.

She had not been able to take to him at all, and neither was she surprised that Gideon had sacked him. It had been obvious to her within hours of her starting work how much he abused his position as Gideon's employee.

Courage had heard the door slam later as he left, but the only reference Gideon had made to the incident had been to tell her coolly the following day that Chris Elliott had 'left'.

Quarrels, arguments and hysterical outbursts in the workplace were not unfamiliar to her—neither was petty theft or even fraud. No wonder Gideon had dismissed the other man without notice.

The phone on her desk rang abruptly. As she reached for the receiver Courage could feel her stomach muscles tensing. Her grandmother's voice sounded distressingly weak as she assured Courage that she felt fine, although rather tired.

'The specialist says that he wants me to stay for another couple of days,' she fretted. 'But it's so expensive, Courage. And...'

'You're not to worry about that, Gran,' Courage quickly reassured her.

She frowned as she heard a helicopter approaching the house. That would be Gideon returning. She didn't want him to come in and find her in the middle of a private telephone call, even one as necessary as this one was...

'I've got to go, Gran... I'll see you tonight...' Her fingers curled anxiously round the receiver as she heard imperious male footsteps outside her office.

'I love you too,' she confirmed chokily to her grandmother as Gideon opened the door and strode in. It was so rare for her grandmother to make any kind of emotional statement that Courage was having to fight back tears as she replaced the receiver.

Was her grandmother beginning to suspect that her condition was more serious than she had been allowed to believe?

As Courage blinked back her tears she heard Gideon saying contemptuously, 'Personally, I've never been a great fan of telephone sex. Especially when it's conducted in my time and on my telephone bill.

'I've brought two guests back with me. They're going to need rooms. *If* you can spare the time from your love-life, of course,' he added sarcastically.

Courage wasn't given the time to correct him. He was already striding out of her office and back down towards the hall.

Automatically she followed him, pausing only to snatch up her suit jacket and slip it on.

His two guests, both male, must have returned with him from Kuwait, Courage guessed. They were both dressed in long, flowing robes, but when Gideon introduced her to them their accents, like their bearing, were emphatically British public school and, Courage guessed, probably Sandhurst.

Smiling, she offered to take them to their rooms, firmly maintaining the kind of eye-contact with them that stressed that the only kind of approach from them she would respond to was one connected with her job. She had learned very early on in her career just how to convey to men that she would not welcome any kind of sexual approach from them.

It didn't take long for her to settle them into their rooms. Her offer of afternoon tea refused, she made a mental note to alert Jenny to their arrival and go over a suitable menu with her. She would also have to check with Gideon to find out how long they were staying.

Her heart sank as she realised that her evening visit to her grandmother would probably have to be cancelled.

She found Gideon in his office, gathering up some papers. It had transpired from the visitors' conversation that Gideon intended to take them round the experimental glasshouses where he developed and tested the special blends of grasses he was constantly working on and improving.

'Only the one night,' was his response when she asked him how long they were staying. 'Not long enough for you to make much of an impression on them, I'm afraid. Although I should have thought that a woman of your age and...experience would be well aware that while they might be quite happy to enjoy your sexual favours, they almost always marry within their own culture.'

Somehow or other Courage managed to bite back the furious retort that sprang to her lips. How dared he judge her so unfairly—and *why* was he doing so? She shrugged the thought aside. She had far more worrying things to think about. Like her grandmother, for instance.

As she smothered another yawn, to her relief Courage heard the sound of Gideon's guests crossing the way and going upstairs.

Thank goodness for that. Now at last she could go home.

Although Gideon had not specifically asked her to stay, she had felt that she ought to do so. It was now almost two o'clock in the morning... A quick phone call to her grandmother earlier had explained the position, and now all Courage wanted to do was to go home and get some sleep.

'Why don't you stay here tonight?' Jenny had suggested when Courage had refused her offer to stand in for her. 'There's a spare bed in my room.'

'I can't,' Courage had told her. 'I need to go home to change my clothes.'

'Well, I can't offer to lend you any of mine,' Jenny had chuckled. 'You can't be more than size ten and I'm a good sixteen.'

So far Gideon had said nothing about Alfonso's replacement, but it had given Courage a great deal of quiet satisfaction this evening to see the surprised approval with which Gideon's Kuwaiti guests had reacted to the appearance on the dinner table of the Kuwaiti dishes she and Jenny had chosen.

The coffee-pot had been drained, too, of its thick dark coffee—only a raised eyebrow from Gideon signifying any reaction to the fact that he had been provided with his own pot of his preferred blend of coffee.

'Why don't you come in a bit later in the morning?' Jenny had suggested, when Courage had told her that she would stay on to see to things.

'I wish.' Courage had grinned ruefully. 'No, I'll be here before seven, as usual. There shouldn't be any problem with the breakfasts, but just in case...'

Now, picking up her bag, Courage headed for the door, pausing to turn round and snap off the light as she opened it.

The sound of someone walking towards her made the fine hairs on the back of her neck prickle.

She turned round warily, her heart thudding against her ribs as she recognised Gideon's tall frame emerging from the shadows beyond the corridor.

'Still here?' He frowned as he looked at her, before checking the time on his watch. 'It's gone two...'

'I didn't want to leave until your guests had gone to bed,' she told him.

His eyebrows lifted. 'That's taking devotion to duty a bit far, isn't it?'

'It's part of my job,' Courage pointed out calmly to him, but the effect of her businesslike statement was spoiled by the unexpected yawn she couldn't quite control.

'You're not intending to drive home, are you?' she heard Gideon demand curtly.

'It only takes half an hour,' she responded. 'And the roads will be quiet.'

She had obviously said the wrong thing, because his mouth had thinned ominously. Without another word he turned on his heel and headed for his office.

Smothering another yawn, Courage walked towards the hallway and the front door. She was just about to open it when she saw Gideon crossing the hallway.

When he opened the door for her, at first she thought he was simply anxious to see her off the premises and set the alarm, but then she realised that he was following her outside.

'This way,' he told her peremptorily when she would have headed for her own car, gesturing instead to the Range Rover parked several yards away from it.

Uncertainly Courage stared at him.

'Get in,' he told her as he unlocked the passenger door for her. 'There's no way you're in any fit state to drive,' he added flatly. 'You're damn near asleep as it is...' His mouth compressed again, leaving her in no doubt as to how he viewed her overtired state—she was a responsibility he would quite plainly rather not have had.

'It's all right. I'm perfectly able to drive,' she told him defensively, but he was obviously not going to listen to her, and to judge from the impatient snort of disbelief her defiance had received he was perfectly capable of physically putting her in the Range Rover if she refused to get in willingly.

Uncomfortably she walked towards it. He had no need to look so angry with her, she decided crossly. *She* wasn't the one who was insisting that she needed driving home... Tired though she knew she was, she *was* perfectly capable of driving.

So capable, in fact, that as she moved to get into the Range Rover she could hardly lift her feet high enough to make the first step.

Her whole body flushed with mortification as she heard another impatient mutter from Gideon.

The house's security lights had flooded the gravel parking area with bright light, but there was still something about the intimacy of being alone with him in the middle of the night that was making her heart pound far too fast... Or was that simply tiredness?

'Here...' she heard him saying curtly, and before she could stop him she felt him virtually lifting her into the Range Rover. His hands were either side of her waist, his fingertips fanning out right up to her ribcage so that he must be able to feel the frantic, erratic thud of her heart.

She could feel the warmth of his breath on the back of her neck. It sent a hot, sharp shiver running all the way down her spine.

Praying that he hadn't noticed it, she kept her head bent as he released her, leaving her to put on her seatbelt while he walked round to the driver's side of the vehicle.

'There really is no need for you to do this,' she protested again as he climbed in and switched on the engine. 'And I'm going to need my car in the morning...'

'Get a taxi and charge the cost to petty cash,' he told her angrily. 'Of course, none of this would be necessary if you were living in.'

'I can't live in,' Courage reminded him. 'My grandmother needs me. That was the whole point of my moving back here.'

She could see that Gideon was frowning as he reversed the Range Rover and then headed for the drive and the main road.

'Your grandmother... Yes... How is she, by the way?'

His question brought all the anxiety and concern Courage had been holding at bay during the day rushing back.

Biting down hard on her bottom lip to suppress the lump forming in her throat, she told him chokily, 'I don't know... She's in hospital at the moment having tests. I had hoped to go and see her this evening... It seems that they may have to do more tests than they originally expected. I won't really know any more until I've spoken to the specialist.'

'She's actually in hospital?'

'Yes... I...'

'Then you'd better take tomorrow off and go and see her.' Before Courage could start to object he added grimly, 'There's no point in you coming to work suffering from both over-tiredness and anxiety... You'll be more of a liability than an asset.'

Numbly Courage turned her head away from him and stared out of the window into the darkness, fighting to blink back her tears. His blunt, almost cruel comment had robbed his earlier apparent generosity of any real warmth or concern for her.

But then, why should he feel concern for her? And why should she care one way or another? Why should it bring her close to the edge of tears to know that the reason he was giving her some time off wasn't one of kindness but because he judged that she was, as he had put it, more of a liability than an asset?

It was just tiredness and anxiety over Gran that was making her feel so emotionally vulnerable, she assured herself shakily. That was all.

It was very warm inside Gideon's car, and there was something about being driven by someone else through the darkness of the silent countryside that made her feel... She searched for the right words to describe the unfamiliar feeling that was filling her. Pampered...protected...cared for... All of the feelings which, for an independent woman, no matter what name you gave to them, were highly dangerous.

Surreptitiously Courage glanced at Gideon. He was concentrating on his driving, barely aware, or so it seemed, that she was even in the car with him.

He was the last kind of man she wanted to feel emotionally drawn to; her instincts told her that. But she felt so alone... So afraid for Gran and for herself.

'You'll need to give me directions from here,' Gideon informed her as he drove through the small village closest to her grandmother's home.

As she did so, Courage was disconcerted to hear the soft, almost tremulous note in her voice.

It was a relief when Gideon finally pulled up outside the cottage, but to Courage's dismay, instead of simply driving off, Gideon climbed out of the car, making it plain that he intended to accompany her right up to the front door.

'It's all right... I...I can manage,' she started to protest, but Gideon was already opening the gate for her, a deep frown etched between his eyebrows as he studied the silent, empty countryside around the cottage. Courage could see the expression on his face quite clearly in the illumination of the cottage's security lights—a precaution she had insisted on having installed for her grandmother, despite the latter's protest.

'How far away from your nearest neighbours are you here?' Gideon asked her grimly.

'A-about a couple of miles,' Courage told him. 'Why?'

'If I were your grandmother's specialist I doubt that I'd want her moving back to somewhere so isolated until I was sure she was well and truly recovered from her operation.'

Courage made no response. It was something she had been worrying about a great deal herself. She *couldn't* be with her grandmother twenty-four hours a day, and they certainly couldn't afford a private nurse, and her shoulders slumped dejectedly as Gideon's comment reminded her of the anxiety she had tried to put to the back of her mind until she needed to worry about it.

It felt odd, walking along the narrow garden path with him beside her. In the night air the scent of the old-fashioned rambling rose that covered the front porch was sweetly strong. A shower of petals covered Gideon's shoulders as he lowered his head to walk under the low porch lintel.

It was dark inside the porch, Gideon's tall frame blocking out the light as Courage fumbled inside her handbag for her house keys, mentally cursing herself for not getting them out beforehand.

If only Gideon wouldn't stand so close to her. She could smell the scent of his skin, and the intimacy of that awareness was causing a discomfiting reaction within her body. She could feel her nipples tightening, swelling slightly against her cotton bra. Embarrassed colour burned her face as she bent her head, still searching frantically for her keys. Where on earth were they?

'Look, there's no need for you to wait. I'll be fine now,' she told Gideon jerkily, forced into lifting her head to look at him.

There was just enough light for her to see his face. She looked into his eyes, her own widening, her mouth suddenly going dry as her glance slid helplessly from his eyes to his mouth.

Without knowing she was doing so she swayed slightly towards him, overwhelmed by the unwanted burden of her own emotions, a telltale shudder visibly galvanising her body.

She stiffened instinctively as she felt Gideon's hands grip her arms as he closed the gap between them, his head lowering towards her own, his mouth seeking hers with the same precision and much the same fatal effect as a heat-seeking missile reaching its target.

That the explosion on impact was within herself, invisible and almost totally silent, apart from one soft, shocked gasp, made it no less devastating for her.

Never in her whole life had Courage experienced such a deeply sensual and experienced kiss. The knowledge in the lips caressing hers held a dark, dangerous allure, a hint of bitterness that sent tiny warning signals darting through her nervous system.

But they were too weak to withstand the power of the male possession of Gideon's mouth.

If she had unwittingly initiated the kiss, there was no doubt about which one of them controlled it now. Courage felt as pliable and formless as a piece of fluid silk, moulded and shaped by Gideon's power into whatever he wanted her to be.

She could feel her heart hammering against her ribs as he drew her against his body, one hand resting against the nape of her neck, caressing her, the other...

Suddenly realising what she was doing...what she had unwittingly invited...Courage broke the kiss, pushing Gideon away.

He released her immediately and, unlike hers, his breathing sounded perfectly composed and level, Courage noticed humiliatingly as she turned away from him, trying to hide her flushed face and trembling body.

As she moved she heard her keys rattling in her coat pocket. Quickly she removed them and turned to insert them in the front door.

What on earth had possessed her to behave so stupidly? No wonder Gideon was watching her with that look of cynical disdain in his eyes.

She very much doubted that she was the first woman to have virtually thrown herself into his arms and invited him to kiss her.

As she stumbled over a hurried goodnight, and let herself into the house without waiting for him to make any response, she wondered what he would have said if he had known that it had not, in fact, been him she had been yearning for... not him she had been kissing. That what had actually motivated her had been the memory of having been kissed once before in the shadows of a night-silent garden, and that just for a heartbeat of time she had ached so much to recreate that past memory that she had allowed her emotions to overwhelm her common sense.

The real cause of her disastrous behaviour was not so much being alone with Gideon in the darkness of her grandmother's porch, she told herself contemptuously, as the fact that for some unknown reason her body and her senses still continued to respond to an unfounded belief that they *recognised* him, instead of more sensibly accepting that they were wrong in confusing him with a man—*the* man—for whom they still yearned so foolishly.

Well, they must surely have learned their lesson now. There was nothing remotely similar in the way that *he* had kissed her—with passion and need, with tenderness and awe—and the way Gideon had kissed her... Nothing at all.

'Courage...'

Courage halted her footsteps obediently as she heard the voice of one of her grandmother's oldest friends.

'How is your grandmother? It seems ages since we last saw her.'

'She's in hospital at the moment, Lady Sara,' Courage explained, adding soothingly when the older woman started to express concern, 'Just for tests at this stage, so that the specialist can establish just exactly what's wrong.'

Lady Sara and her aunt had been friends for many years; they were both on the same charity committees and they played bridge together. Courage had often visited their home with her grandmother and now, knowing how much her gran would hate too much fuss being made of her illness, she deliberately played down its seriousness to the older woman.

'Will you be able to stay for very long, or is this just a brief visit?' Lady Sara asked her.

'Well, actually, I'm working locally now,' Courage told you.

'Are you? Where?'

'Hettingdean Manor...'

'What? You mean you're working for that dreadful Reynolds man?' Lady Sara demanded, aghast. 'He's not the sort of person you should be working for at all, my dear. A young man—the nephew of some friends of friends of ours—was employed by him for a while and he treated him most dreadfully...'

Courage frowned. She knew that Lady Sara and her husband, Sir Brian, had been on Gideon's invitation list for his cancelled dinner party, and she suspected that she also knew who the nephew of the friends of friends was.

'Well, I haven't worked for him for very long, but so far I haven't any complaints,' Courage told her lightly, firmly dismissing from her mind the memory of last night's kiss.

That had been a mistake, and one she simply wasn't going to dwell on or repeat. She couldn't afford to, could she...? Not while she owed Gideon so much money. Money which, for her grandmother's sake, she simply could not repay.

'Of course, it's different for a woman,' Courage added. 'Gideon Reynolds is very successful—and very wealthy. That's bound to cause a certain amount of resentment among his own sex...'

'Oh, yes... Of course... Quite...' Lady Sara agreed. 'He is very much a self-made man, though, isn't he?' she added questioningly.

'His fortune is self-made,' Courage agreed. 'And certainly he doesn't make any secret of that fact. But then I rather tend to admire that in a person. He's a very sophisticated and intelligent man.'

'Oh, I see… I rather had the impression that he was… Well, something of a rough diamond…'

'On the contrary,' Courage assured her. 'And then, of course, his business does bring him into contact with… I don't want to go into too much detail, but I believe he was contacted by a member of Prince Charles' staff about a special environmental project the Prince wanted his advice on…'

Lady Sara was, as Courage had known she would be, properly impressed by this information, although she did look a little confused.

'An environmental project…? But I thought… That is…we understood that he…that his business was mainly concerned with the supply of guns—all that sort of thing!'

Now it was Courage's turn to be surprised. No wonder Gideon's dinner invitations had been refused if that was the sort of rumour that had been spread about him.

'Good heavens, no,' she said firmly now. 'He's actually an expert in landscape architecture.'

'Really?' Lady Sara looked very impressed. 'In that case Brian would no doubt love to meet him. He has been complaining all summer about the state of the south lawn… He's tried everything, but there's still a huge bald patch right in the middle of it. I must tell him what you've said, Courage. In fact, we really ought to invite Mr Reynolds over to lunch… Do give our love to your grandmother, my dear… How long will she be in hospital? I'd like to visit her.'

'I'm not sure, but I'll get in touch with you and let you know once I've seen the specialist,' Courage offered. 'I'm just on my way to see him now.'

'Oh, yes, please do…'

Well, at least she had solved the mystery of why local society had refused Gideon's invitations, Courage decided as she hurried towards the entrance to the hospital. She ought to have guessed it would have something to do with Chris Elliott.

She had little doubt that Lady Sara would be as good as her word and invite Gideon over for lunch. But whether or not he would thank *her* for her interference on his behalf, if he ever got to know about it—which, if she had anything to do with it, he most definitely would not—was another matter. Because Lady Sara was notoriously mean and would no doubt expect him to pay for his lunch by giving Sir Brian free advice about his lawn.

A wryly amused smile touched her lips, but it disappeared very quickly as she glanced across the road at the bulk of the hospital.

The specialist had sounded very serious when he had rung her at home this morning, asking her to call and see him after she had seen her grandmother.

It was just as well that Gideon had given her some time off, even if his generosity had caught her off-guard.

That was twice now that he had gone out of his way to help her, and yet she still had the feeling that somehow there was something about her that he almost actively disliked. But if that was the case, surely he wouldn't have employed her in the first place. She was being hypersensitive, she told herself firmly.

The real problem was probably the fact that she did not like being so deeply in debt to him. It would have worried her knowing that she owed *anyone* such a very large sum of money and she was constantly aware of it.

It was the sound of a motorist's car horn blaring warningly at her as she unwittingly stepped out into the road without looking properly that made Courage realise what she was doing.

Apologetically she stepped back on to the pavement.

She was still in a state of semi-shock, she acknowledged. Her grandmother had looked so well when she had gone in to see her that to hear the specialist tell her so gravely that the tests had revealed her condition to be far worse than they had first suspected had hit her like a sickening blow in the stomach.

'The problem is that this particular condition is highly unpredictable. It can remain static for years then suddenly accelerate for no apparent reason. In your grandmother's case... Well, let's just say that in terms of world-class athletics its acceleration would have qualified it for a gold medal.'

He had waited sympathetically for Courage to take in what he was telling her.

'How... how much time does she have?' Courage had asked him shakily, once she was able to speak.

'Without an operation...?' He had shaken his head. 'Not very long at all, I'm afraid. But that is the dark side of the picture. Your grandmother basically has a very strong constitution, and we know that this particular operation, although complex and lengthy, does have a very high success rate. There is no reason why, once she has fully recovered from it, she should not go on to enjoy one and possibly two more decades of good health.

'A lot, of course, will depend on the way the post-operative period is managed. I should very much like her to go into a specialised nursing home for at least a month, possibly two months, after the operation.'

'Two months...' Courage had whispered, wondering how on earth she was going to manage to cover the extra expenses that that would cause...

'I'm sorry to have to give you such bad news,' the specialist had told her. 'But try to look on the bright side. As I've already said, this particular operation has a very high success rate. Obviously, in view of the deterioration in your grandmother's condition, we will want to keep her in and schedule the operation just as early as we possibly can.'

'When?' Courage had asked him, dry-mouthed.

'Possibly the end of this week, or maybe the beginning of next,' he had told her consideringly. 'We want to stabilise her system as much as we can first, and that will mean putting her on a course of special drugs.'

'Have you told her? Does she know?'

'Not yet,' the specialist had informed her. 'I wanted to speak with you first.'

'Can I...? I...I want to be with her when you tell her,' Courage had insisted firmly.

'Yes, of course,' the surgeon had agreed.

To Courage's relief her grandmother had taken the news far better than she had expected. Her system had still contained some of the sedatives they had given her before doing the tests, the specialist had informed Courage.

Whatever they were, she wished she might have some of them, Courage decided shakily now, as she double-checked before attempting to cross the road a second time.

She felt uncomfortably light-headed and nauseous, her brain thick and woolly with all the information she was trying to assimilate. Tears of shock and fear clogged the back of her throat. The last time she had felt this afraid and alone had been just after that incident in the garden...

Afterwards Courage was never quite sure how she managed to drive safely from the hospital to Hettingdean Manor, or why she had chosen to go there instead of going back to her grandmother's cottage.

When she walked into the kitchen Jenny took one look at her white face and pain-filled eyes and immediately steered her into a chair, demanding, 'What is it? What's happened?'

Still in a state of shock, Courage told her.

'Well, at least it sounds as though the specialist believes the operation will be a success,' Jenny tried to comfort her.

'Yes,' Courage agreed. 'I'm being silly, I know. It's just, I hadn't expected...'

'You've had a bad shock,' Jenny told her, stopping speaking as the kitchen door suddenly opened and Gideon strode in.

At first he didn't see Courage, and said, 'Jenny, forget about Sunday lunch will you?' Courage heard him continue, with a far warmer and more friendly inflexion to his voice than she was used to hearing, 'It appears that I've been invited to have lunch with Sir Brian and Lady Sara instead. Although I doubt——'

He stopped abruptly in mid-sentence as he suddenly caught sight of Courage.

'What are you doing here?' he demanded, frowning down at her. 'I thought I gave you the day off...'

Ignoring her pleading look, Jenny was already tactfully whisking herself out of the room, but the very last thing Courage wanted right now was to be left alone with Gideon.

'Did you visit your grandmother?'

'Yes,' Courage told him, and then to her absolute horror her eyes filled with tears, her throat closing up under the overwhelming force of the emotions that threatened her.

'What is it...? What's wrong...?'

Gideon was still frowning at her.

Courage could hear the irritation in Gideon's voice, but she couldn't bring herself to look at him.

'My...my grandmother's condition is more serious than the specialist first believed,' she told him stiltedly. 'He's...he's going to bring the operation forward...'

'And?' Gideon persisted.

Courage didn't want to answer him but she knew she had very little alternative.

'The...the operation has a very high success rate...' she said quietly.

'What's going to happen to your grandmother after the operation?' Gideon questioned her, ignoring her shaky statement.

'After the operation?' Courage stared blankly at him. Right now she was far too concerned with the operation itself to worry about the problems she would have to face afterwards, but Gideon's question reminded her that they would have to be faced.

'She...I don't know... The specialist wants her to go to a special nursing home...'

'How long for?' Gideon was almost snapping the question at her, his voice as savagely sharp as the incisors of an animal.

'I...I don't know... A month...maybe two...'

'Sounds expensive.'

Courage shot him a haunted, tormented look.

'Money. Is that all you can think about?' she demanded bitterly. 'My grandmother——'

She checked herself but it was too late.

'Your grandmother, what?' Gideon pressed grimly on.

Courage shook her head.

How could she explain to him how much her grandmother meant to her, how much she loved her...? How much she needed her, how much she felt she owed her?

'I'll find the money,' she told him fiercely instead. 'Whatever it takes, whatever I have to do.'

The last thing she wanted was for him to think she expected or wanted him to lend her any more. She had seen the cynical, almost bitter expression in his eyes when he had made that comment to her about her grandmother's recuperation being expensive.

Why on earth had she come back here in the first place, instead of going straight home? She watched him as he walked past her, her face flushing scarlet with mortification as he turned round and she realised that she had been staring straight at his mouth.

CHAPTER SEVEN

'COURAGE, have you got a moment, please?'

Uneasily Courage followed Gideon into his office.

'I've been thinking... Since your grandmother is unlikely to be living at the cottage for at least the next two months there's no reason why you shouldn't move in here. It would certainly facilitate things from my point of view if your hours were more flexible,' Gideon continued, without allowing her to speak.

'As you know, I'm due in Cornwall tomorrow. Then I'm off to Kuwait and we've got the Japanese arriving next week. I've promised the Duchy of Cornwall people that I'll let them have an outline plan by the end of the month—they'll probably want to come up here to discuss it.'

Courage knew that what he was saying made sense. Some evenings it was close to midnight before she left and it would be far less tiring to make her way to one of the apartments in the stable-block than to drive all the way home.

'I... I'm not sure——' she started to say, but Gideon was already standing up.

His, 'Good, that's all settled,' drowned out the hesitant protest she had been about to make.

'Your grandmother's operation is scheduled for tomorrow, isn't it?' he asked her as he held the door open for her.

'Yes,' she agreed.

He had already offered her the day off, but Courage had refused. She would much rather be working than simply sitting around waiting...feeling helpless... Unable to do anything to aid her grandmother.

She was going to see her this evening and would visit her again after the operation, just as soon as the specialist said she could.

Gideon had still not replaced his sacked PA and Courage had found that she was taking on more and more of his old duties and, in so doing, working far more closely with Gideon than she had originally anticipated. The work itself she found fascinating and challenging, but the man who generated it...

Whether because of the emotions reawakened by the sound of his voice or because of the man himself, she didn't know, but there was something about even the most businesslike proximity to Gideon that made her feel tautly on edge, not wholly in control of herself or her responses.

It still brought a hot flush of shame to her face to remember how she had responded... almost *invited* him to kiss her the evening he had driven her home.

She was under no illusions... A man like Gideon, even without his wealth, would attract scores of women. It would be no new thing to him to have a woman flirting with him, encouraging him to make love to her.

For the first couple of days after the incident she had worried almost obsessively over what he must be thinking of her, but her concern for her grandmother had now taken the place of that more intimately personal concern.

'You might as well move your things over here today. There's no point in delaying...'

Courage tensed. She hadn't heard Gideon walking into her office.

'No,' she agreed hollowly. She knew it made sense for her to live in; she had, after all, done so when she'd worked in the hotel trade, so it wasn't anything new to her. So why did she have this feeling of reluctance... of unease, almost, about doing so? She would have Jenny for company, after all.

'I didn't realise you knew Sir Brian and Lady Sara.'

Warily Courage waited a few seconds before saying as lightly as she could, 'Lady Sara knows my grandmother.'

'Of course. I should have realised...'

Courage frowned at the cynicism she could sense beneath the outward smoothness of his voice.

'I believe I have you to thank for my lunch invitation last Sunday.'

Now she could *hear* the hardness in his voice. It made her flinch slightly, although she tried to hide her reaction from Gideon's sharp eyes.

'I simply corrected Lady Sara's false belief that you were some kind of arms dealer,' she told him, as calmly as she could.

'An arms dealer?' His eyebrows shot up. 'Why on earth should she think——? Ah...yes, of course. No doubt I have my late and lamented personal assistant to thank for that piece of meddling. Why did you do it?'

'Why did I do what?' Courage asked him, pretending not to understand...

'You know what I mean. You had no need to say anything to her—you could have let her go on socially ostracising me...'

'I didn't like what Chris had done,' Courage told him, looking squarely at him, her chin firming, her eyes wide and serious. 'It was mean and dishonest, and totally unfair...'

She saw that Gideon was frowning at her.

'I'm sorry,' she apologised. 'You obviously don't think I should have interfered. But I hate that kind of behaviour, that kind of small-mindedness and meanness, the kind of person who takes pleasure in putting others down...in hurting them——' She broke off, her face flushing as she realised how emotional and intense she sounded. 'I doubt you'll think I've done you much of a favour in the long term. Sir Brian is bound to ask you for your advice about his lawns and——'

'He already has,' Gideon told her wryly.

There was a glint of rueful amusement in his eyes that made Courage drop her guard enough to ask curiously, 'What did you tell him?'

'The truth. That the entire lawn should be dug up and the ground re-seeded. I also told him that if he wanted to consult me professionally I could let him have a list of my consultancy fees ...'

Courage choked back a small gasp of laughter.

'That won't have made you very popular,' she warned him.

'No,' he agreed. 'But the days are gone when I'm prepared to be tolerated simply for what people can get out of me ... I won't *buy* their acceptance.'

The wintry look in his eyes made Courage shiver slightly.

'Not that Sir Brian's given up,' he added. 'They've invited me over for dinner next month. Lady Sara suggested that you might partner me ...'

Courage gave him a flustered, uncomfortable look.

'Oh, no. I couldn't. You wouldn't——'

'So I'm good enough to work for... but not good enough to be seen socially in public with, is that it?' he asked.

Courage stared at him.

'No... No, it isn't anything like that,' she denied, shocked both by the anger in his voice and the sentiments he had expressed.

'I ... just ... I thought ... It doesn't seem very fair of Lady Sara to foist me off on you like that.'

'Very tactful. But I suspect what you really mean is that it isn't very fair of her to foist *me* off on *you*. Do you really think I don't know what people like that say about me behind my back? "Not quite our sort, my dear,"' he told her savagely, mimicking the upper class drawl of Sir Brian and his friends. '"Plenty of money, of course. Pity he doesn't have the breeding to go with it..."'

'Do you know what I was doing while people like you ... like Chris were going to your nice, expensive private schools, while you were secure in your expensive, carefully protected, upper class worlds? I was working with a gang of navvies, building motorways, lying about my age, always on the move so that the Social Services people wouldn't catch up with me and put me back in one of their "homes".

'I was thirteen when my mother died. My father had left home long before that. He didn't want us... didn't want to know. My mother did her best, but she didn't have the heart for it once he'd gone. You don't get much of a start in life living in a condemned block of flats.

'After she died the council put me into care. Care... My God... I ran away... three times. After the third time I swore I'd never go back. Luckily I was big for my age and could just about manage to pass for sixteen. When the motorway contract finished I was out of work for four months and then I got a job working for a——' He broke off suddenly, frowning down at her. 'What the hell am I telling you all this for?'

Go on, Courage wanted to urge him. Tell me more... Tell me everything.

The pain and anger in his voice as she listened to him had touched her emotions so intensely that she felt close to tears. She could almost feel the anguish he must have experienced at his father's desertion; his mother's fear... *his* fear and misery when he was placed in the home, his loneliness. She wanted to reach out and touch him... To hold him...

The shock of what she felt made her body tense in rejection. The feelings she had just experienced were almost those of a woman in love... A woman wanting to comfort the man she loved.

The man she loved... In love with Gideon Reynolds...? Impossible. She would *never* allow herself to be anything so foolish... so dangerous.

In love with Gideon Reynolds... She gave a small shiver. Of course she wasn't.

She knew very well what was causing her to be so emotionally and physically aware of him, she acknowledged grimly. It was her own fault. If her own memory had not played that silly trick on her, making her think for that split-second of time that his voice was that of another man, none of this would ever have happened.

But it had happened, and by some alchemical and unfathomable means it had somehow opened a secret, hidden door deep within her psyche, which had made her dangerously vulnerable to Gideon as a man.

She gave a small involuntary shiver. What made the whole thing so much worse was that she suspected that Gideon, with that predatory male sensuality which he possessed in such abundance, was equally aware of her vulnerability.

Nothing had been said, but once or twice she had seen him looking at her, watching her, his glance resting just that fraction of a second too long on her face or her body, in a subtle underlining of her femaleness and his maleness.

Jenny had noticed it too, once commenting to her teasingly, 'I think our boss rather fancies you...'

Courage had immediately denied it, but her face had gone pink and she hadn't quite been able to meet Jenny's amused gaze.

'Don't knock it,' Jenny had advised her. 'He's a real hunk, and for once—and this happens rarely—I'll bet he'll be even better as a lover than he looks.'

She had apologised when she had seen how embarrassed Courage was.

'I'm sorry. I forget sometimes how young you are, Courage. At your age you still quite rightly believe that emotional love and sexual desire are things that go hand in hand. At my age... Well, let's just say that by then you've suffered enough disappointments to know how rare really good sex is and to appreciate it when you do find it. And I'm certainly glad I'm not young enough to fall in love with Gideon myself. There's a certain hardness about him, a cynicism that could prove very hurtful to the woman who loves him.'

Courage fully agreed with everything that Jenny had said. Even when Gideon was being 'nice' to her she was still conscious of sensing that somehow he was masking his real feelings, that deep down inside he did not really like her. And yet she had no real base for that feeling. Nevertheless, it disturbed her, and it was always a relief when Gideon went away on business.

Tiredly Courage let herself into her small self-contained apartment above the garage block. She had just come from visiting her grandmother—her first visit since the operation—and even though she had known from a telephone call from the specialist that the operation had gone well, she had still been anxiously on edge, unable to believe fully what he had told her until she had seen her grandmother for herself.

She had come through the operation extremely well, the specialist had told Courage, and he was extremely pleased with its success.

However, he had warned Courage that it was crucially important now that her grandmother received the right kind of post-operative care.

If she kept her own living expenses to the absolute minimum, and used her grandmother's pension income, Courage estimated that she could just about cover the cost of her grandmother's recuperation. But in doing so she would be unable to make any repayments for the loan Gideon had made her.

Knowing that she would have to approach him to discuss the matter was weighing heavily on her—but what else could she do?

There was no other way she could find the money to finance her grandmother's recovery, and as it was... She grimaced as she looked down at her bare legs. Thank goodness it was summer and she was spared the expense of having to buy tights—that was how stretched her finances were going to be for the next two months.

As she kicked off her shoes, and padded barefoot into the apartment's tiny kitchen to make herself a cup of tea, she reflected that it was just as well that Gideon was away on business. Somehow, she just didn't feel able to cope with the trauma and stress of her grandmother's operation and Gideon as well...

Not that he hadn't been generous about giving her time off to visit her grandmother—even to the point of insisting that she was to feel free to ignore the demands of her work and visit the hospital as frequently as she wished.

Of course she was grateful to him, but at the same time she was also conscious of the fact that his generosity put her under an even greater burden of debt to him. She might not be able to make any inroads into repaying the money he had loaned her at present, but she was certainly going to make sure that her work didn't fall behind. Even if that did mean, as it had for the last few days, that she would be working late into the night to make up the time she had taken off during the day to be with Gran.

Gideon was due back later this evening and she wanted to have her desk cleared of its backlog of work before he arrived.

CHAPTER EIGHT

COURAGE had just stepped out of the shower and was reaching for a towel when she heard someone knocking on the apartment's outside door.

She frowned as she wrapped the towel sarong-wise round her body. It couldn't be Jenny, as she had decided to use her time off to go and visit her daughter.

Warily Courage padded across the carpeted living-room area of the apartment, glancing through the small window into the courtyard outside as she did so.

She could see Gideon's car parked outside the garage. Her heart beating unsteadily, she unlocked the door and opened it slightly. Gideon was standing outside.

'I was just on my way to bed,' she told him unsteadily.

He had obviously only just arrived back. He was still wearing a formal business suit and tension lines were etched either side of his mouth, caused, no doubt, by his drive back from Cornwall. Courage had heard on the news earlier that there had been a hold-up on the motorway due to some roadworks.

'So I see.'

The look he gave her as he swept her body from head to foot in a deliberately detailed sensual scrutiny made Courage curl her toes protestingly into the soft carpet, but instinct warned her not to protest or acknowledge that she was aware of the taunting provocation of what he was doing. There was an air of dangerous tension about him that put her own nerves on edge.

'I won't keep you long. I just wanted to go over the arrangements for the Japanese visit with you.'

'N-now?' Courage stammered. 'But...'

'I'll be leaving for Kuwait tomorrow,' Gideon reminded her, 'and I expect you'll want to visit your grandmother. How is she, by the way?'

He had taken hold of the door as he spoke, pushing it open so that Courage had no option but to give way and let him in.

The small apartment was far more luxurious than the type of accommodation she was normally used to—in most of the hotels where she had worked she had counted herself extremely lucky to have her own shoe-box of a room. Here she had a comfortably sized double bedroom, a shower-room, a good sized living-room and a small kitchen—more than enough space for her.

But somehow now, with Gideon in it, the room seemed to have shrunk so much that there was nowhere for her to go without having to walk unnervingly close to him; it even seemed as though there was barely enough oxygen for the two of them to breathe, or at least that was what her lungs were telling her as they fought to take in enough air, her chest and throat suddenly constricting.

'She...she's come through the operation very well,' she told Gideon. 'The specialist is very pleased with the way everything went...'

'But?' Gideon stressed, his eyebrows lifting queryingly as he frowned down at her.

'There is no but,' Courage denied. She wanted to pick her own time to ask him if she could delay starting the repayments on his loan, and this was most definitely not it. Not when he had caught her off-guard and she was feeling so vulnerable... Not when all she had on was a soft and now very damp towel, and she was all too conscious of the way her body was reacting to his presence beneath its uncertain protection.

No. When she had to approach him about the loan she wanted to be fully in control of the situation and of herself. But there was something she *did* have to say now, she acknowledged.

Gideon had walked over to the fireplace and was studying the silver-framed photograph she had placed there of her grandparents and her father. Anxious to keep as much distance between them as she could, Courage backed away from him until she felt the edge of the sofa cushions preventing her from going any further. It was only just a little over a metre, but at least it was better than nothing, Courage decided, as she cleared her throat and began nervously.

'I still haven't thanked you properly for lending me the money to pay for Gran's operation. I really am grateful to you and...'

'Are you, now? Just *how* grateful, I wonder? Let's just find out, shall we? You can thank me now.'

Too stunned to speak or move, Courage stared at him in confused shock as he came towards her, his movements as dangerous and purposeful as any four-legged predator.

As he took hold of her her reactions came too late and were far too little, just a helpless little moan of protest immediately stifled by the hard pressure of his mouth. The hands she lifted to fend him off were dealt with just as ruthlessly, both her wrists held captive by one hand while he used the other to pull her even more closely against him and keep her there.

Angrily Courage tried to push him away, her eyes darting fiery sparks of fury into the hard sexuality of his.

Oddly she felt no sense of fear, only an adrenalin-driven flood of emotion cresting dangerously unfamiliar excitement.

Excitement because she knew she was engaged in a battle she could only lose. Excitement because of knowing how perilously little chance she had of withstanding the explicit demand of Gideon's fiercely male kiss, and excitement because she knew in her heart of hearts that this... that *he* was what she wanted.

A tiny shudder convulsed her body and then another, her lips parting in helpless response to the probing demand of Gideon's tongue.

She felt his hands on her body, searching for and finding the end of her towel and then tugging it free with a gentleness that would have surprised her had she been in any state to pay attention to such things.

As it was, the brief sensation of cool air against her skin meant only that she was completely naked—and the sudden swelling of her breasts and tightening of her nipples had nothing to do with any drop in the temperature and everything to do with the fact that she knew that Gideon was looking at her and that soon he would be touching her.

That she, who had always been modest to the point of prudery about her body, should be filled with this desire to have Gideon look at her was a disconcertingly startling experience.

She shuddered again, this time more intensely, her own eyes widening as she saw the glitter in Gideon's as he looked at her.

'No...'

The protest was instinctively protective, as was the step she took away from him, but she had forgotten that the sofa was immediately behind her and that there was nowhere for her to go.

'Yes,' Gideon told her softly.

He was still looking at her...her eyes...her mouth...the intensity of his gaze mesmerising her, making her shiver helplessly.

She was looking right into his eyes when he raised his hand and very deliberately drew a slow circle around one nipple with the tip of his finger.

Courage's body reacted as violently as though he had poured a thousand volts of electricity into it, her face, the whole of her body flooding with betraying heat as her eyes betrayed to him just how sensually sensitive she was to his touch.

'You want it,' Gideon told her thickly, still holding her gaze. 'You know you do...'

Courage closed her eyes, unable to withstand the look he was giving her and unable to deny his statement either.

She had never felt like this before. Never. It was like being held tight in the grip of a need so savage that it was almost a pain—the kind of pain that could drive you to madness, to becoming an aching, needing, hungry, empty body of flesh beneath the hands of the man who generated those emotions.

Her knowledge of what was happening to her shocked and appalled her. Where was the strength she needed to fight it? Why was she simply succumbing to the dark, dangerous undertow that was sucking her down into waters far too deep and dangerous for her to survive in?

Gideon's fingertip traced another circle and then another around her nipple.

Without having to look at it she knew it was hard and swollen, echoing the same ache that was pulsing so heavily deep down inside her body.

There was something wanton—pagan, almost—about being with Gideon like this, completely naked and vulnerable to what he was causing her to feel while he remained fully clothed, distant from her. Almost at the same time she could sense his own fiercely controlled physical desire.

'You like that, do you...? You want me to do it again...? Well, I want *you* to do *this*,' he whispered against her ear as he took hold of her hand and placed it low down on his body.

Instinctively Courage recoiled, trying to snatch her hand away, but he kept it pressed against the hard heat of his arousal.

This kind of intimacy, this type of caress... It was for teenagers, surely—groping frantically at one another in the darkness while they could—not for adults, Courage felt. Somehow she had thought that Gideon was not the kind of man who would want to be touched like that—that he would hold himself aloof from this sort of thing. But while her mind rejected what he was telling her he wanted to do her senses, her body, her traitorous fingers seemed to find the sensual contact with his flesh dangerously exciting.

So exciting, in fact, that when Gideon began to move closer to her, slowly kissing his way along her jaw, cupping her face in both of his hands as he caressed the exquisitely sensitive spot just behind her ear, his fingertips stroking her skin, she started to make soft, frantic mewing sounds of mingled pleasure and frustration deep down in her throat. Her senses were dominated by her need to touch him more closely, more intimately, without the barrier of his suit.

Nothing remotely like this had ever happened to her before.

Only once before in her whole life had she experienced this kind of need...this kind of arousal.

Her whole body suddenly went still, her eyes widening. She saw Gideon raise his head and look at her.

What she was doing wasn't right... It was a betrayal of all her most private dreams. To give in to the sexual desire he seemed to ignite inside her with such demonic skill would be a desecration of everything she held most dear.

She opened her mouth to tell him so, and then closed it again on a stifled sob of shocked pleasure as Gideon bent his head to her breast. With nerve-wrenching, slow deliberation he ran the tip of his tongue around the flushed aureole of flesh, and then over and over its hard, aching tip, until the swollen skin was bathed in moistness and Courage was moaning softly under her breath, her back arching in mute demand, her nails digging into his shoulders as she silently willed him to put an end to her torture and suck the scorching, throbbing need from her.

When he finally did so a sensation so physically intense that her body shuddered violently in response to it ran like a fiery cord from her breast to her womb, contracting her body with such fierce waves of pleasure that they made her cry out in shock.

'It must be a hell of a long time since you last had a man, if that can bring you to orgasm,' she heard Gideon muttering rawly against her mouth, as he released her breast to kiss her and pull off his clothes.

'Well, you might have had yours, but I've still to have mine. So I hope you'll understand if I revert to type and don't behave like a gentleman,' he told Courage roughly, as he stepped free of his clothes and reached for her.

She might have had her orgasm, as Gideon had said, but that didn't appear to mean that her body was satiated. Far from it, Courage recognised only seconds later, as Gideon picked her up.

Just the lightest friction of his body hair against her breasts was making her whole body tremble, while the knowledge of how close the hand he had curled round her thigh was to the warm, wet centre of her body...

The thought of how she was going to feel once he was inside her was making her dizzy with excitement and longing.

'I always knew you'd be good,' Gideon told her softly as he pushed open the bedroom door and carried her over to the bed.

As he placed her on it he lowered his head and circled her navel with his tongue. The hand which had been caressing her thigh now slid between them, not touching her, just holding still while Gideon lifted his head and looked into her eyes.

Her own gaze faltered beneath his and slid away down his body; a hot shudder rippled through her as she focused helplessly on his manhood.

She didn't *need* experience to tell her how she would feel once Gideon was inside her, how he would fill and pleasure her. After all, in her dreams she had already known this intimacy with him many, many times; in her dreams she had already felt the heat and passion of him, touched and caressed him, known the pleasure of holding him deep within her own body.

Dizzily Courage tried to cling on to reality, to reject the emotional trap her body was setting for her—trying to confuse her by pretending that Gideon was her dream lover... He was no such thing. He was...

As Gideon started to touch her, his fingers stroking tantalisingly against her, she exhaled her pent-up breath on a small, frantic moan. What did reality matter anyway...? What did anything matter but this...? Gideon and what he was doing to her.

'God, you're wet. You're so wet that you feel like you are ready for me now... Are you, Courage? Do you want me...? Do you want to open your legs and wrap them round me, draw me deep inside you?

'Take care, though,' he warned her as he started to move against her, slowly stroking himself inside her. 'I don't want to disappoint you, to leave you aching and unsatisfied. That's a very special kind of hell, isn't it? It makes you lie awake at night, aching for someone who isn't there. Has anyone ever made you feel like that, Courage? Somehow I doubt it. You're not the kind of woman who allows her lovers to disappoint her, are you?'

Her lovers... Courage froze, her body tensing, panic and pain flaring simultaneously through her as what he was saying shocked through her, pain abruptly replacing pleasure as reality threatened the fragile cloak of her self-deception... What lovers?

She saw Gideon frown as he felt her body tighten around him and fight him.

'Stop it,' he warned her, tight-lipped. 'It might flatter the egos of your other lovers to pretend that you're still a virgin, but don't play the virgin for me. It does nothing for me. And besides, I know the truth.'

Courage gasped as she felt the swift, sharp stab of pain overwhelm her body. But, even as she was reacting to it, it was gone, her shocked muscles responding to the hypnotic rhythm of Gideon's ever-deeper thrusts. A feeling—the same feeling she had experienced as he sucked on her breasts—was gathering deep inside her body, and with it a compelling sense of urgency that drove her, possessed her...

Sleepily Courage stretched languorously against the male hands caressing her body, smiling in the darkness as her body recognised and welcomed the touch of its lover.

As she raised her arms to draw him closer, she sighed in soft, drowsy satisfaction.

This eager welcoming of his body by hers, this silent, night-covered perfect meshing of their bodies was, after all, nothing new to her; she had known it a thousand times and more in her dreams. Just as she had known him, would have known him anywhere—the scent of his skin, the way he moved, the way he held her...touched her. All of them had been recorded so faithfully and in such detail by her sensual memory that they were instantly recognisable.

She murmured happily in soft appreciation as his hands stroked over her skin, touching him in return, tracing the smooth column of his throat with her lips, feeling the fierce upsurge in his heartbeat.

Once, long ago in a dark, shadowed garden, she had wanted to touch him like this, had trembled in awe and excitement when he touched her. Had wanted him, ached for him, with a need and hunger that had been as pure and innocent as she had been herself.

Then she had been too shy, too overwhelmed by the shocking intensity of her own feelings to respond to them. Now...

She heard the low, masculine sound of pleasure he made as she touched him, felt him move his body invitingly against her hand.

He was a stranger to her, a man she had known once briefly, very briefly, when the reality of her own womanhood had still been a mystery to her. A man who even now in so many ways was still a stranger to her, and yet somehow it was as though her body—*their* bodies—were so sensually familiar and pleasurable to one another that they automatically moved together in perfect harmony.

The words Gideon had used to her, the harshness in his voice, which had confused and hurt her, had become unimportant when he touched her and held her. No man could give a woman so much pleasure and risk the pain of her potential rejection when he invited her to do the same for him without feeling some emotion.

There was no doubt in Courage's mind or heart now, as she lovingly pressed herself against him, inviting the possessive invasion of his body, welcoming the full power of the deep thrusts which she had initially nervously rejected, that Gideon was the man she had been tricked into meeting in her parents' garden, and it was that knowledge that set her gloriously free of the inhibitions and reservations which had previously imprisoned her sexuality.

Then, all those years ago, she had been cheated of the natural and longed for conclusion to their lovemaking. Now...

She shuddered in timeless ecstasy as she felt her body slide helplessly under the spell of Gideon's pulsing rhythm and start to match it...

When she woke up it was daylight and Gideon had gone, but her body and her bed still carried his scent and she closed her eyes, luxuriating in recreating the feel and presence of him.

Gideon and the man who had made love to her so intensely, so heart-stoppingly that she had never been able to forget him, never been able to let any other man take his place, were one and the same.

She should have trusted her instinct over that phone call, she acknowledged sleepily. If she had...

They must have been destined to be lovers... No wonder she had been so strongly sexually attracted to him.

Were *his* memories of her as strong as hers of him? She frowned, opening her eyes. If so, why hadn't he said something? Did he, perhaps, not remember her at all...? Could he even have *forgotten* all about her?

She shivered slightly, steely little ice-picks of doubt piercing the sleepy pleasure of her daydreams.

What if to Gideon she was just another willing bed-partner? What if she meant nothing to him as a person at all? What if all those special dreams...those tender, loving thoughts...that special knowledge which had made the pleasure of being loved by him and loving him in return so much more than a merely physical coming together had not been something which he had shared at all?

Hadn't she herself refused to believe what her senses were telling her at first, convinced that the stretching of coincidence so far simply could not happen?

After the euphoria of the night's emotional and physical heights, the feeling that filled her now was like a sickening, swift fall back to earth.

Of course Gideon had recognised her. He must have done... His body must have known, just as hers had done...

But what if it hadn't...? All those years ago she had not been the girl he had expected to have in his arms...the girl he had wanted to have there.

Last night she hadn't allowed herself to acknowledge the fact. Last night she had been so caught up in her own emotions and desires that she had simply assumed that Gideon shared them too.

Certain things he had said, the tone of his voice when he had said them, now came back to her. Things which last night she had chosen to ignore as unimportant, things which in her own emotionally heightened state she had simply dismissed as negligible, no longer seemed quite so easy to dismiss in the cold light of day.

'You can thank me now...' Gideon had told her, and later, as they had made love, she had assumed that he had meant that she could thank him with her love... But what if he had not meant that at all? What if he had meant something completely different and far, far less intimate and loving?

The trouble was that she had no previous experience to go on... No awareness of what men did say in the heat of their desire.

'Don't play the virgin for me,' Gideon had told her harshly, but the actions of his body as its possession had adapted to the shocked tension of her body had seemed to mitigate his words, and she had thought it unnecessary to tell him that she was not playing, that her virginity, while not, perhaps, something she was exactly proud to admit to, was nevertheless a fact. Not so much because she had made any conscious effort to retain it, but more because her body had never wanted any other man in the way that it had wanted his younger self.

What was she doing looking for problems, when by rights she ought to be walking on cloud nine?

Her grandmother was safely over her operation and Courage had just found the man who had invaded her dreams and possessed her most secret self ever since she had first met him. A man whom she had thought never to meet again.

If only he was with her now. She ached to hold him. To talk to him. To tell him how ashamed and afraid that long-ago evening had made her. How worried she had been for him, how guilty about her part in what had happened.

'Don't worry,' her grandmother had soothed her. 'I'm sure the young man, whoever he is, will have realised that you were as much a victim of what happened as he was himself.'

She had taken comfort from her grandmother's wise counsel then, but now she ached to reassure herself that Gideon had not suffered from the incident.

A wry smile curled her mouth. Her stepfather and his daughter would no doubt be extremely surprised and chagrined if they ever learned how successful Gideon had become. For herself, his financial success was unimportant. It was Gideon himself who mattered.

Gideon... Gideon... She closed her eyes, mentally working out how long she would have to wait to see him again. Funny how things had turned out. Had it only been yesterday that she had told herself that it was a relief to know he was going away, that she preferred it when he wasn't there...? Now...

The mystery of why she had been so intensely aware
of him, her emotions and her body so intensely disturbed by him, was solved.

Her emotions had known what her body and mind
had refused to recognise.

Suddenly she ached for him to be with her, to be able
to talk to him, to ask him...to explain to him. He
couldn't have recognised her, she decided reluctantly,
because if he had he would surely have said so.

Which meant that it was up to her to remind him of
that long-ago meeting, even if that did mean that she
had to face the pain of discovering that he could not
even remember the event.

She didn't want their relationship to start with any
shadows between them, any old ghosts, even if *she* was
the only one who was aware of their existence. Honesty
had always been important to her, in every aspect of her
life, but most especially where such a very special and
intimate relationship was concerned.

What would he say when he discovered that she had
not, in fact, been 'playing' the virgin? A small, gentle
smile curled her mouth. She would perhaps not tell him
that yet, but wait until their relationship was a little better
established, a little more equally balanced, before sharing
with him the knowledge that she, the young girl of long
ago, had been so overwhelmed by him, by his mascu-
linity, that he had become her dream lover, and that her
body had steadfastly clung to its longing just for him.

He would laugh, of course, and so would she. But
deep in her heart Courage knew that a part of her, a
small, secret, deeply female part of her, would always
be glad that he had been the first. And the last?

Only time knew the answer to that question.

'What's brought that smile to your face?' Jenny quizzed
her teasingly, later in the day when they were both in
the kitchen, Jenny having returned from her visit to her
daughter. 'Anyone would think you've fallen in love.'

Courage couldn't help it; she could feel her face flooding with brilliant colour, even though she shook her head and denied Jenny's assertion.

Even when she had been with her grandmother she had been guiltily aware that her thoughts kept returning to Gideon as she wondered what he was doing and if he was thinking of her.

The specialist continued to be pleased with her grandmother's progress and was proposing that she was moved to the convalescent home within the next few days.

'All this fuss,' her grandmother had sighed, but she had not argued or protested.

Never had so few hours seemed to last for so long, Courage decided achingly later that night, lying awake in her bed thinking of Gideon, longing for him, wanting him. Was it really only twenty-four hours since she had lain in Gideon's arms, had held him and been held by him... had loved him and been loved by him...? With almost a tortured moan she turned over, burying her hot face in her pillow.

Gideon. Gideon... If only he were here with her now... If only...

She felt almost dizzy with her emotional and physical longing for him, her skin burning alternately hot and cold with feverish desire as she closed her eyes and gave in to the temptation of mentally reliving the events of the previous evening. The way he had held her...touched her... The stroke of his fingers against her skin... The heat of his mouth... The girl she had been would have been shocked by the raw intensity of his sexuality, but the woman she now was...

Oh, Gideon... Gideon...

CHAPTER NINE

BY JUGGLING with her work and conscientiously making sure she had made up the time by working well into the evening, Courage was able to take enough time off to go with her grandmother to the convalescent home recommended by the specialist, and to see her comfortably settled in her new, temporary surroundings.

'Honestly, all this fuss,' her grandmother complained. But the stress of the operation had taken its toll on her and she did not protest too much when the nurses insisted that she had to rest.

'Heaven knows what all this must be costing,' she fretted to Courage.

'You're not to worry about anything like that,' Courage told her firmly. 'Leave everything to me. You just concentrate on getting yourself better.'

'It's just as well we operated when we did,' the specialist had told Courage earlier. 'The damage was even more extensive than we had suspected. Your grandmother is a very strong woman and a very stubborn one. I suspect she must have been suffering a great deal more than she wanted to acknowledge, and I doubt she could have continued on for very much longer.'

'But she'll be all right now?' Courage had pressed him anxiously.

'Right as rain,' he had reassured her. 'Provided she behaves sensibly and gives her body time to recover properly, which is one of the reasons why I want her to have this extended period of recuperation.'

Courage had felt so relieved she had almost been lightheaded. She still hadn't discussed delaying the repayments to her loan with Gideon, of course, but she was sure that once he knew what had happened he would understand.

In view of their new relationship, it was even more important to her than ever that she maintained her financial independence. It was one thing to have accepted a loan from Gideon as her employer, but now that things had changed ... now that they were lovers ...

She prayed that he would have the sensitivity and understanding not to suggest giving her the money. Her pride and her self-respect had always been very important to her, and while she could appreciate that he might want to help her, and that to him a sum of money which might seem enormous to her would be trifling, she very much wanted to stand by their original agreement.

Asking him to accept a delay in the commencement of her repayments on the loan was not what she really wanted to have to do—it hurt her pride to have to go back on her given word—but her grandmother's health and well-being were more important to her than her pride.

Her heart started to beat faster. Important though it was, discussing the repayment of her loan with Gideon was not exactly going to be her first priority when he did return. A delicate flush stained her skin as she remembered the morning she had taken his breakfast into his bedroom and she mentally reran the whole scene, imagining that it was taking place now and not then.

When she came to the bit where Gideon had appeared wearing only a towel her thoughts were so intensely sensual and erotic that she could actually feel physical reaction to them within her own body.

How many hours now until Gideon came back?

However, when he did return it was not the exciting, intimate event Courage had anticipated. To start with he telephoned while she was out on a restocking trip combined with a fleeting visit to her grandmother and told Jenny that he had been delayed in Kuwait in consultation with a potential new client whom he would be bringing back with him. They would return in time for lunch the next day, he further told Jenny, and his client would be staying overnight.

'Looks like he could be getting quite a lot of business in Kuwait and in the neighbouring Middle Eastern countries,' Jenny commented.

'Mmm. The Gulf War caused so much destruction out there, it's not surprising, really,' Courage agreed firmly, swallowing her own feeling of disappointment and letdown.

There would be time enough for her and Gideon to be alone and talk once his client had gone, and he was, after all, only staying the one night, she comforted herself. That was all.

In the meantime there was work to be done, and her training came to the fore as she went over the menus with Jenny and then went upstairs to check on the guest-suite which was being prepared for Gideon's client.

On the day of Gideon's return she had been up early to go to the market and buy the fresh supplies Jenny needed and to get freshly cut flowers for the house and the guest-suite.

She arranged them deftly while Jenny looked on in admiration.

'You make it look so easy. I love those natural, soft arrangements so much more than the old-fashioned, stiff variety, but whenever I try anything like that it just doesn't work.'

'It's just a matter of practice,' Courage assured her, standing back to check on the display she was working on in the huge fireplace which dominated the hallway.

The pale creamy colour of the lilies and the froth of soft green and whites she had used with them complemented the rich colour of the dark wood.

By lunchtime the scent of the lilies would have filled the room. Courage loved displays that were scented— freesias in spring, roses in summer, the rich, warm scent of spices mixed with the ashy smell of burning wood in winter, the earthiness of ripened fruit in the autumn, displayed in huge bowls of rich gold and russet colours, highlighted by the darkness of newly picked plums with the bloom still on them.

Wherever possible, Courage preferred to see flowers and fruit indigenous to the area in her arrangements, and the lilies were very similar to those she had seen growing in a sheltered part of the house's garden.

In the dining-room a huge bowl of massed sweet-peas broke up the plain crispness of the white damask tablecloth.

Courage glanced at her watch, trying to subdue the butterflies tormenting her stomach.

At one-thirty, when Jenny came into her office to ask her anxiously if she had heard anything from Gideon as she was concerned that lunch would spoil if it was kept waiting much longer, Courage was glad of her training to fall back on as she dealt calmly with the older woman's anxiety without revealing that she herself had been counting almost the seconds since twelve o'clock, her ears stretched for the returning sound of Gideon's car, her heart pounding, her whole body going dizzy with longing as she anticipated the moment when he would walk in and she would see him again.

At two-thirty she agreed with Jenny that an alternative cold meal would have to be organised for lunch, and at three-thirty she had already been on to the airline to try and find out if she could trace which flight Gideon had been on.

None of them had any record of him travelling as a passenger on their Kuwait to Heathrow flights.

In the end it was gone five o'clock before Courage's ears caught the sound they had been straining for all day—Gideon's voice outside in the corridor as he talked to the prospective client he had brought back with him.

As he opened her office door Courage felt her heart start to lift in happy pleasure. The urge to leave her desk and run towards him and throw herself into his arms was so intense that she wasn't quite sure how she managed to avoid giving in to it. As it was, she couldn't quite control the smile quivering round her mouth, nor the soft light warming her eyes as she saw him walk into the room.

'Courage, are you responsible for those lilies in the fireplace?'

The abrupt, almost accusatory tone of his voice froze her smile, confusing her and extinguishing the happy glow from her eyes.

'Yes. I——'

'Then come and remove them, will you? My client is allergic to their scent...'

Mortified, Courage started to apologise, her face flushing as guiltily as a naughty schoolgirl's as she turned to follow Gideon, who had already turned on his heel and walked back into the corridor.

He was walking so fast that she almost had to run to catch up with him.

'I'm sorry, Maryam. I'll have the damn things removed immediately,' she heard him saying as he turned the corner and walked into the hallway ahead of her.

Maryam...

Courage's heart missed a beat and then another as she, too, turned the corner and saw the woman standing by the hallway's circular table.

She was tall and dark-haired, her olive skin as smooth and silky as her polished hair. She was wearing a neutral-toned trouser-suit with a plain silk-satin blouse, both of them very obviously Italian in design and more than likely from Armani's couture range, Courage guessed.

She had seen wealthy Arab women before on many occasions, and had often been wryly touched to see the expensive finery they wore concealed in public by their traditional robes, but this woman had an air of self-confidence and self-assurance about her that said that there was no way she intended to obey anyone's rules other than her own.

Her jewellery, like her make-up and her clothes, was awe-inspiringly expensive and very subtly discreet. She was closer to Gideon's age than her own, Courage guessed, and from the brief but dismissive look she had given Courage herself not a woman who considered any other members of her sex to be any threat to her.

'I'm sorry about your flowers,' she apologised to Courage in perfect English. 'Unfortunately I am allergic to their scent... If someone could show me to my room?' she added to Gideon, turning away from Courage in dismissal. 'After that delicious lunch all I want to do is sleep, and I have some telephone calls I must make home to Baraq... My father-in-law worries so...'

She gave a small shrug. 'It is a result of the atrocities against our family, of course. For a man of his age to have seen his own sons die... I had hoped that encouraging him to take an interest in his gardens again might help him, but as you saw for yourself... It is very sad. But Baraq is a small country, and we do not have men with your design expertise, so now I'm afraid you will have to work with me...'

Courage could feel the fine hairs at the back of her neck lifting in atavistic jealousy as she heard the flirtatious note in the other woman's voice.

'I'm already looking forward to it...' she heard Gideon respond, equally sensually.

Courage's hands shook as she started to remove the offending lilies from her arrangement, her eyes threatening to film with tears. How could Gideon flirt with another woman after what they had shared...? Didn't he realise how much he was hurting her...? How horribly jealous he was making her feel.

'Which room have you put the Princess in, Courage?' she heard him asking her.

Swallowing back her pain, she replied as calmly as she could. 'Shall I go with——?' she began, but Gideon cut her short, saying that he would show the Princess up to her suite.

Courage refused to give in to the temptation to turn round and watch them as she heard their feet on the stairs. Was Gideon walking alongside the Princess, as the width of the stairs allowed? His hand beneath her elbow, perhaps, as he politely guided and helped her... Was she smiling at him, standing as flirtatiously close to him as she could, letting her body just touch his, watching him from beneath mock-demurely lowered eyelashes—using all the feminine charms that women of her culture were taught to make the most of from birth? Eastern women laughed at European women like her for their refusal to make full use of the weapons nature had given them, Courage knew.

Even after they had disappeared the powerful scent of the Princess's perfume continued to fill the hallway, easily dominating that of the now condemned lilies.

Courage's tender heart mourned their unexpected death-warrant while they were still in the first flush of their fresh beauty. She touched the petals gently in mute apology to them for the role she had unwittingly played in their early demise.

Gideon had made no reference to the fact that he had not returned in time for lunch, as he had arranged, but it was obvious that he and the Princess must have lunched somewhere from her conversation.

The Princess was a business client of Gideon's, Courage reminded herself firmly; that was all. There was no reason for her to feel so insecure and jealous... Would she have wanted Gideon to take her in his arms in front of the other woman? No, of course she wouldn't, she accepted. But nevertheless there was a forlorn and unhappy droop to her mouth when she finally removed the offending lilies, and she could not quite stop herself from glancing towards the stairs. Gideon and his guest were still up there somewhere... Together...

'Wow, that Princess Maryam really is something else,' Jenny commented forthrightly, rolling her eyes slightly when Courage called in to see her late that night on her return from her evening visit to her grandmother. 'I thought Middle Eastern women were supposed to be docile and retiring...'

'Not when you're a member of the ruling royal family,' Courage told her wryly.

She had discovered the Princess's status during dinner, although why on earth Gideon had insisted on her joining them when the pair of them had barely had a word to spare for her throughout the meal, she really had no idea.

She had learned also that the Princess was a widow, and that her husband and brother-in-law had been killed during the Gulf War.

After dinner the Princess had announced that it was far too early for her even to think of going to bed, and had persuaded Gideon to take her out to a night-club. Not that he had needed very much persuading.

Courage had been on her way out herself when she had seen the pair of them crossing the hall. The Princess had been wearing a body-hugging black and silver full-length evening dress which showed off her figure to perfection. But it had been the sight of Gideon, looking impossibly, sensually male in a formal dinner-suit, that had made her heart lurch achingly against her ribs. She had had to bite down hard on her bottom lip and turn away from the sight of the pair of them together.

The Princess was simply a business associate of Gideon's, she reminded herself again, and if Gideon had appeared to be ignoring her since his return, well, she was probably just being over-sensitive.

But somehow her reassurances had rung rather hollowly in her own ears, and now, learning from Jenny that Gideon and his guest had still not returned, she was filled with fresh misery as she pictured the pair of them dancing together—Maryam held in Gideon's arms; Maryam dancing intimately close to Gideon's body; Maryam enjoying the attention, sharing the intimacy that *she*, Courage, had been aching for...

It had been Maryam's suggestion that they went out, Courage reminded herself fair-mindedly, not Gideon's.

It had been bad enough longing for Gideon when he wasn't there, but somehow this was even worse.

Don't be silly, she chided herself, as she said goodnight to Jenny and walked the short distance to her own apartment. Gideon would never have made love to her if she hadn't meant something very important to him. He simply wasn't that kind of man.

Her hotel work had shown Courage the tell-tale signs that betrayed a man who was a heartless womaniser. But there had been no mysterious telephone calls for Gideon while he was away, no eager female voices demanding to speak with him, no request to her to send flowers or make hotel and dinner reservations. In short, none of the signs which would have revealed a casual, careless attitude on his part to emotional or sexual intimacy with her sex.

Of course, there were bound to have been other relationships in his life, she knew that.

What kind of relationship would the one they shared be? Her heart missed a beat and then started to hammer frantically against her chest wall. She knew what kind of relationship she wanted it to be: the kind that involved wedding-rings and making vows, the kind that included having children—several of them—the kind that involved celebrating their silver wedding together and hopefully their gold, the kind that involved love—not just on her part but on his as well.

All at once her eyes filled with tears. She wanted so much to be with him, to talk to him, to be held by him while she confirmed her love to him, while she admitted to him how often she had thought of him over the years. How often she had dreamed of him and yearned for him . . .

It was gone two o'clock before Gideon and the Princess returned. Courage was just on the point of falling asleep when she heard the car, followed by the sound of doors slamming and then the Princess's laughter. Plainly *she* had enjoyed her evening. Had Gideon enjoyed it as well, or, like her, had he secretly been longing for an opportunity for *them* to be alone together? Courage wondered.

She held on to that comforting thought as she tried to get back to sleep, but it was no real compensation for Gideon. He was the one she really wanted to be holding on to and to be held by.

Her stomach quivered as her body reacted to the thought of sharing such intimacy with him, of lying next to him, sleeping in the same bed... Waking up to the warm drift of his hands over her body, knowing how much he wanted her... how much he loved her.

At least the Princess would not be staying long, Courage comforted herself. She had learned over dinner that the reason she had not been able to trace any record of Gideon's return to Heathrow on a scheduled flight had been because he had flown back on the Princess's private jet, and that she had business in New York in connection with her late husband's estate, which meant that she would have to leave the following afternoon.

Courage had never thought of herself as an insecure or jealous woman before, but then she had never felt for any other man what she felt for Gideon. Had never loved any man, never ached or yearned for any other man the way she now did for Gideon.

Determinedly she tried to banish from her mind the tormenting image of the Princess. Tomorrow Maryam would be gone. Tomorrow she and Gideon would be alone and able to talk.

Tomorrow... Tiredly she slid into an uneasy sleep.

CHAPTER TEN

'GIDEON not back yet...? Looks like he's taking his time saying goodbye to Her Highness. Not that she'd have any objection to that. From the way she was looking at him over breakfast this morning it was pretty obvious that she'd rather have been sinking her teeth into him than into my croissants.'

Jenny laughed and then stopped, frowning as she saw Courage's expression.

'Is anything wrong?' she asked her in concern. 'Is it your grandmother? Has something...?'

'No, Gran's fine,' Courage mumbled, turning her head away from her. How could she tell Jenny that it had been her comments about the Princess which had upset her?

'Are you sure?' Jenny persisted, obviously not convinced. 'I know I said I'd have this evening off, but I can always cancel my arrangements and stay if——'

'No... no, you mustn't do that,' Courage told her. 'I... I'm probably just feeling a little bit stressed from the build-up to Gran's operation. Even though everything's gone well, I...'

'I know exactly what you mean.' Jenny agreed comfortingly.

'If you're going to make it to London in time for your theatre date, you'd better go and start getting ready,' Courage warned her.

'You're right,' Jenny agreed as she glanced at her watch. 'Are you sure you don't mind? It's just that my friend booked the tickets months ago, and...'

'Of course I don't mind,' Courage assured her firmly.

'I've left some cold salmon and a salad in the fridge, and there's some raspberry mousse and——'

'Go and get ready,' Courage interrupted her.

Food was the last thing she wanted. She was too nervous...too on edge...

Nervous... On edge... At the thought of seeing Gideon—of being alone with him... A small frown crinkled her forehead.

Surely that nervousness should really be excitement? That edginess a deliciously wanton sensual tension? The words she had chosen suggested that she was apprehensive about seeing Gideon rather than eager.

Some old friends were visiting her grandmother this evening, leaving Courage free to catch up on her work, and since it wasn't the cleaning team's scheduled day to come in, and rather than have the added expense of an extra visit to put down on her accounts, Courage decided to clean through the Princess's room herself.

It wouldn't take long. After all, it was only a matter of stripping the bed, removing the flowers and the used bed-linen and towels, checking to make sure that the Princess hadn't left anything behind and then leaving the rest until the cleaning team came in the following day.

Courage smiled a little ruefully to herself as she mounted the stairs, heading for the guest-suite the Princess had occupied. These good housekeeping traits of hers, which her Swiss employers had always admired and praised, had their roots in her grandmother's insistence that there was no point in putting off a job or in making extra work for oneself. 'Clean as you go' had been the motto she had instilled in Courage as a teenager.

It had been a hot, sultry day, with the threat of thunder hanging in the air all through the afternoon, and after she had finished her office work Courage had showered and changed into a pair of patterned black and white leggings and a short, sleeveless white square-necked top which, while not provocatively or fashionably midriff-revealing, was still boxy enough to allow a welcome current of air to touch her skin.

Outside the door to the guest-suite the Princess had used, she hesitated warily. What was she afraid she would find inside? Evidence that Maryam and Gideon had spent the night together? The imprint of two heads on the pristine white pillows instead of one?

What was wrong with her? She already knew that Gideon was not sexually or emotionally promiscuous. Just because he had allowed Maryam to flirt with him over dinner it did not mean that he had gone to bed with her.

The huge wave of sick misery that drenched her at the thought of Gideon—her Gideon—even smiling at the other woman, never mind anything else, shocked her. She wasn't used to having these kinds of dark, self-punishing thoughts. Why in the world should she think that Gideon would want anyone else? She ought to be feeling happy, excited, not filled with anxiety and pain.

It was because their relationship was so new, she comforted herself. She would feel better once they had talked—once she had told Gideon about her past...their past... and the role she had unwittingly played in her stepfather's abuse of the authority he had had over Gideon. She, after all, had been tricked by her stepsister just as much as Gideon himself. The guilt she had carried with her all down the years was the guilt of a frightened child, fearful of somehow being blamed for the wrongdoings of others.

As her grandmother had said at the time, Gideon had no doubt very quickly realised that Courage had been just as much of a dupe in the game that her stepfather and sister had played with one another as he had himself.

There had been many, many times over the years when she had wondered what had happened to him after he had been dismissed by the firm who employed him, but she had never come anywhere near guessing the truth.

She opened the door and walked into the bedroom. The large double bed pillows bore the imprint of only one head, she noticed, her face flushing slightly even though she was alone in the room as she quickly turned her head away.

The rich, expensive scent of the Princess's perfume still hung heavily on the air, causing Courage to wrinkle her nose slightly and immediately head for the windows to open them. Perhaps to a man such a powerfully strong scent was sexy, but Courage found it too strong and cloying.

Damp towels littered the bathroom floor, and when Courage went to pick up the wastepaper bin, prior to emptying it, she was startled to see that it contained the Princess's discarded underwear—the briefest of push-up bras in delicate silk and a minuscule matching tanga. The two together had probably cost more than she spent on her underwear in a decade, Courage reflected as she removed them from the bin and put them on one side for laundering and returning to their owner.

She sympathised with the Princess in not wanting to carry worn linen in her luggage, but to throw them away... What it must be like to be so rich... And yet Courage did not really envy her.

Carefully placing the Princess's underwear on top of the used towels, so that they didn't accidentally get mixed up with them, Courage checked the bathroom for anything else the Princess might have left behind and then returned to the bedroom and started to strip the bed.

Outside, the early evening sky had turned a dull sulphur colour, and she could hear thunder growling in the distance. Would Gideon return this evening, or would it be tomorrow before she saw him? He had given no indication of when he intended to return—perhaps he might even decide to stay overnight in London. The thunder was coming closer, and lightning zigzagged across the sky, a handful of huge raindrops exploding against the window-pane without doing anything to dissipate the heavy, sultry atmosphere.

The guest-suite was at the back of the house and had an excellent view of the grounds and the hills far away in the distance. As she went to close the window against the rain Courage thought she heard a door slamming somewhere else in the house.

She frowned, wondering if there was another window open somewhere, and then went back to her self-imposed task of neatly folding the sheets she had just removed from the bed.

She was still engaged in this task, her back to the closed door, when it suddenly opened, and she whirled round just in time to see Gideon come striding in.

Immediately the sheet was forgotten, sliding from her fingers, and her face was alight with her emotions as she moved impulsively towards him, exclaiming happily, 'Oh, Gideon, you're back... Oh, I'm——'

'What the hell are you doing in here?'

The harsh tone of his voice confused her. She looked uncertainly at him. 'I was checking the room and——'

'Checking it—what for?' Gideon was frowning as he looked round. Courage saw his frown deepen as he focused on the neat pile of damp towels and the underwear on top of it.

'I thought we employed a team of cleaners for this kind of work...'

'We do,' Courage agreed. 'But sometimes guests inadvertently leave things behind, or——'

'And you like to have first pickings?'

Courage's eyes widened as he strode past her and picked up the Princess's discarded underwear.

'And what exactly did you intend to do with these?'

Courage stared at him, totally thrown by his remarks and his anger.

'I was going to arrange for them to be laundered and then returned to the Princess,' she told him, giving him a puzzled look.

What was wrong? Why was he so angry? She took a hesitant step towards him. It must be her imagination, she reassured herself. He couldn't possibly believe, as she had begun to think, that she had actually intended to keep the Princess's thrown-away underwear, like some poor, unfortunate down-and-out searching through dustbins or scavenging for food... The very idea was unthinkable... insulting.

Gideon was looking away from her, staring towards the window. He looked tired, she recognised. Her heart melted with love for him, her emotions overwhelming her. Reaching out tentatively towards him, she touched his arm gently.

'I've... I've missed you,' she told him shyly. 'I...'

He was looking at her now, and her face flooded with soft colour as she saw the way his glance fell from her face to her body and then lingered there. Her heart started to race, a now-familiar yearning ache building up inside her body.

'I... I need to talk to you, Gideon,' she told him huskily. 'There's something I need to tell you... It's... it's rather important.'

If he took her in his arms now she would never be able to concentrate enough to tell him about the past, she recognized dizzily. If he...

'Important!'

The harsh tone of his voice startled her.

'I see. And just what is this "important" conversation you want to have? Or can I guess...? You want to tell me that you can't afford to repay the money you've borrowed from me, that you need more time—is that it?'

Courage stared at him. How had he known about that? A puzzled frown creased her forehead.

'I... I was going to ask you about that,' she admitted. 'But that wasn't what I wanted to talk to you about now.' She took a deep breath. 'I know this might sound... strange, but you and I... we've met before...' Courage paused, risking a brief, appealing glance into Gideon's eyes before looking hurriedly away again and continuing.

'You may not remember. Well, I don't suppose you do. It was a very long time ago and it wasn't—— Well, the circumstances——'

'On the contrary. I remember it very well.'

The hard, incisive tone of his voice checked her.

'You do?' she asked doubtfully. 'But you never said anything. You——'

'Neither did you,' Gideon pointed out.

Courage could feel the hot flush scorching her skin.

'That was because...I didn't really know. I wasn't really sure, until the...the other night.'

'The other night?' Gideon questioned sharply.

'Yes,' Courage admitted.

Gideon had, after all, every right to be angry with her, since he had obviously recognised her right from the start, while she...

'I...I did think I recognised your voice,' she told him huskily. 'But it wasn't until...until you k-k-kissed me that I really knew it was you...It was dark that night—the night we met,' she reminded him shakily. 'I never really saw your face. And——'

'You never saw my face but you recognised my kisses after all this time—all the other men who have undoubtedly passed through your life. Oh, please. Exactly what kind of fool do you take me for?' Gideon interrupted her angrily. 'Not the same one you and your sister set up so easily between you...Do you know what your little piece of fun cost me? Do you? What happened to her, by the way?' he demanded.

'She's...she's living abroad somewhere with her father,' Courage stammered. 'We don't...we don't keep in touch...'

'I see. Decided you'd make richer pickings apart, did you? Or did the pair of you just become too notorious together?'

Courage stared at him. The sick feeling that had invaded the pit of her stomach as she listened to him was growing steadily more crippling, fogging her brain and her thought processes to the point where she could scarcely believe she was hearing what Gideon was saying. Surely it all had to be part of some horrible nightmare? It couldn't possibly be real.

'What...what are you trying to say?' she stammered shakily. 'I didn't... You must understand... I had no idea...'

'Don't lie to me,' Gideon told her. 'You knew, all right. Your stepfather told me all about you after you'd gone. The games you liked to play, the problems he'd had with you, the complaints from your school about your promiscuous behaviour...the embarrassment you'd caused him.'

'That's not true...none of it...' Courage cried out, white to the lips as she stared at him in shocked pain. 'You can't believe it is. I——'

'Can't I? Why not? You came on to *me* strongly enough that night. You were all over me, practically begging for it, and to judge from your behaviour the other night nothing's changed...'

Courage could hear his cruel words, and she knew that later she would feel the pain of them, but right now something—shock, perhaps?—had blessedly anaesthetised her against them, allowing her to stand her ground instead of running away, allowing her to ask huskily, 'Well, if you knew who I was—if you recognised me, as you say—why did you give me a job? Why did you lend me money? Why——?'

'Why do you think?'

'I don't know,' she responded honestly. But Gideon obviously did not believe her. There was an ugliness in the sound of the laughter that followed her response which at any other time would not just have repelled her but almost frightened her as well.

'Oh, come on, you aren't that naïve. Far from it. Oh, I grant you, it must have come as a shock to you to realise who I was... You must have thought you'd fallen well and truly on your feet...found yourself another easy victim. But this time the roles are reversed, and you are the one who is the victim.'

Victim...? What was he talking about? What did he mean? Courage could feel the sweat starting to prickle through her skin as her anxiety increased. She had never felt less worthy of living up to her name.

'Nothing to say for yourself?' Gideon taunted her. 'You've still got one very powerful weapon left, haven't you, Courage...? That sexy, eager little body of yours. How many times have you used it to get what you want, I wonder? Can you even remember?

'How easily and greedily you fell into the trap I baited for you. Accepting my job... accepting my loan; so very foolishly giving me control over your life, giving me the power to make you do as I wish, to punish you as I see fit.

'Can you remember how your stepfather punished me for my presumption in touching his precious stepdaughter?' Gideon demanded bitterly.

Courage shivered, her skin as chilled now as it had been overheated before. Beyond the bedroom windows the sky was still sulphur-coloured as the thunderstorm drew closer, but, threatening though it was, it held far less terror for her than the man standing in front of her.

'You—you employed me out of revenge,' she managed to stammer shakily, trying to inject as much disdain and disapproval into her voice as she could.

'*You* might call it revenge. I call it justice,' Gideon told her. 'Oh, don't run away with the idea that I've spent the last decade and more of my life thinking about you. I haven't. But because of you your stepfather damn nearly ruined my life, and I promised myself then that if I ever got the opportunity to make you pay for what you'd put me through I'd damn well do it. And when you turned up here for an interview and I recognised you, I remembered that promise—that promise I'd made to myself. *You* made it easier for me, of course, with your greed...'

'If by my "greed" you mean the money you loaned me, that was for my grandmother,' Courage reminded him. 'I can't believe you're doing this,' she added, as she fought to swallow back the tears of shock and pain threatening to flood her eyes.

Didn't he realise what he was doing? What he was saying? Didn't he know how wrong he was about her? Couldn't he see...? Hadn't he been able to tell just how inexperienced she really was...? Hadn't he felt her love for him when she touched him, when she welcomed his hands, his body with hers?

'Why not? Have you any idea how much you cost me? My pride...my job...my whole life. Oh, I can understand why your stepfather got me the sack—I don't suppose he wanted me spreading the word about what his precious daughters were really like. He even saw to it that I couldn't get work anywhere else. The firm I worked for refused to give me any references. When my landlady discovered I couldn't pay the rent she threw me out. It was just as well it was a hot summer. It isn't much fun living on the streets...'

He saw the way Courage's face changed colour.

'What's wrong?' he demanded. 'Finally beginning to realise what you did, are you? Well, it's too late for remorse now... Not that I suspect you're capable of feeling such an emotion.'

'But you did eventually get another job?' Courage asked him, ignoring the pain his cruel remarks caused her.

'A job?' He gave a mirthless laugh. 'I got work, if that's what you mean. There are always people who'll employ the vulnerable—they don't have to pay them properly, you see, or follow any health or safety codes. It's all part of the so-called black economy.'

'But you've become successful...rich...' Courage protested, shivering with reaction to what he had told her.

'No thanks to you. I had to work damned hard to get where I am today... Long hard days of backbreaking physical work and equally long nights spent studying. I was lucky... One of the lecturers at the college I attended took an interest in me and got me a part-time job labouring at a local research institute where they were working on some experiments with various grasses for use in semi-desert conditions. I got involved with a lot of the fieldwork they were doing. I was offered a full-time job there, and the opportunity to study for the necessary qualifications to enable me to progress in environmental landscaping and the rest, as they say, is history.

'I must say I was surprised to discover that *you* actually worked. Your father was a wealthy man...'

'My stepfather,' Courage reminded him quietly. How could she tell this man the truth about her upbringing? He obviously wouldn't believe her.

She could understand how he might have formed the wrong opinion of her from what her stepfather had obviously told him about her, even though he must surely have sensed from that brief time which she had spent in his arms just how inexperienced and young she really was, but for him to continue to make the kind of cruel and wholly unfounded remarks about her which he had just made was something she found hard to comprehend. His cruelty had hurt her very deeply, but fortunately the shock of what was happening was so intense that it had almost numbed her, blunting the ferocity of the blow he had dealt her.

Was it for this that she had so carefully cherished her memories of him? Clinging to them for comfort, using them as a measuring-stick against which no other man had ever been able to compare.

'So what is it you intend to do now?' she asked him tonelessly, forcing herself to look directly at him without betraying how much it hurt her to do so. Was that really the face she had caressed so recently? The mouth she had kissed and been kissed by? The eyes which had looked into hers with what she had been so sure was need and desire? 'Sack me...?'

'Sack you?' The sound of his laughter made her cringe. 'Oh, no. You aren't going to escape as easily as all that. Not that it wouldn't be tempting... To throw you out, refuse you a reference, and then sit back and watch you suffer the way I had to. But of course you possess a saleable asset I didn't have...'

A frown crinkled Courage's forehead as she looked at him. 'My training, do you mean?' she guessed. 'But——'

'Your *training*. Oh, come on! You know damn well that wasn't what I meant. I was talking about your body...your sexuality—a commodity which I'm sure you've found very valuable in the past. There are, after all, always men who are willing to pay for the pleasure of having a woman like you. Young...very attractive and highly sexed...'

He ignored the involuntary sound of distress Courage made as she listened to him.

'I expect you've lost count of the number of men who've paid you for the use of those assets. The difference is that this time you will be the one doing the paying. Or rather, you will be the one reimbursing me with your body.'

Dry-mouthed, Courage demanded in a cracked, disbelieving voice, 'You expect me to have sex with you...?'

'Why not? I didn't notice you doing any objecting the other night. Far from it. In fact——'

'That was different,' Courage interrupted him angrily. 'That was when——'

'When you thought I didn't know the truth about you...?'

'You can't possibly mean this,' Courage protested. 'It's archaic... It's...it's inhuman...immoral. You can't possibly really want me...'

'Not cerebrally or emotionally,' he agreed unkindly. 'But as for the rest...' He gave a brief shrug. 'I'm a man, with all the normal man's needs, and right now you're like an irritating little itch that I need to scratch. Fortunately such irritations aren't long-lived, but while they do exist they tend to be extremely demanding and intense...' He had started to pull off his jacket as he spoke and, as Courage stared at him in appalled disbelief, he started to unfasten his shirt.

This couldn't be happening. Gideon couldn't be standing there calmly telling her that he intended to have sex with her as a means of punishing her and humiliating her for something over which she had had no control.

'I noticed from your medical records that you regularly give blood—most commendable—and at least I know that I'm not taking any risks with my health in bedding you. But then I suppose a woman of your experience knows very well how to guard herself against such things.'

'That's a vile, horrible thing to say,' Courage burst out, her face betraying her shock and revulsion.

'Is it? On the contrary. These days anyone—man or woman—with the least degree of responsibility and self-preservation needs to ensure that they are not taking risks with their sexual health and——'

'There are ... there is another risk that we ... that you would be taking...' Courage told him, stammering slightly over the words and praying that they would act as a deterrent to his cynical threats.

'Another risk?' Gideon was frowning at her, his eyebrows lifting slightly in mocking contempt as he realised what she was trying to say.

'A child, you mean? Oh, come on. We both know that you...' His frown suddenly deepened, his mouth hardening. 'But, yes, you are right. It is a risk, and one that would be far more to my detriment than yours. I have no wish to be sued for child support, or to provide you with a meal-ticket for life via an unplanned conception. That could be a tempting prospect to a woman like you...'

Courage couldn't believe her ears. Her face flushed hotly with angry colour.

'How dare you?' she breathed furiously. 'The last thing—the very last thing I would ever want is to conceive your child. *I* am not the one who is planning to force you to have sex with me. And, as far as I am concerned, the one who would suffer most from such a con-

ception would not be you, it would not even be me...
It would be the child... I would never, *never* want to
bring into the world a child who was not wanted or loved
by both its parents.'

Tears started to fill her eyes as her emotions overwhelmed her, and she was so busy blinking them away
that she did not see the tiny, frowning look Gideon gave
her, as though something about her passionate speech
confused him slightly.

'Your acting talents are very impressive, but in this
instance completely wasted,' he told her grimly after a
few seconds' pause. 'But, now that you have reminded
me of the danger, I can promise you that *I* shall take
whatever steps are necessary to ensure that there is no
risk whatsoever of your conceiving my child. As I just
said, in such circumstances I would be the one who stood
the greater risk, and I should perhaps be grateful to you
for unwittingly reminding me of it. Women—some
women,' he amended, 'are notorious for becoming
"forgetful" over their birth-control precautions when it
suits them. But if you were planning——'

'*I* was not planning anything,' Courage interrupted
him hotly. '*You* are the one... I can't do this. You can't
make me... I *won't* let you...' she told him, her voice
starting to rise semi-hysterically.

'Very well, then,' Gideon told her silkily, lifting his
hand away from his half-unfastened shirt. 'In that case,
I want full repayment of the loan I made you, plus
interest. Immediately...'

'You can't do that...' Courage protested, white-lipped.

'You should have read the contract,' Gideon taunted
her. 'If you had, you'd know that I can.'

Courage wet her over-dry lips. 'I can't repay you...
I don't have that kind of money...'

'Very well, then. I shall just have to apply to your
grandmother for it,' Gideon told her carelessly.

'No... No, you can't do that...'

'You can't repay me, and you don't want me to approach your grandmother. That doesn't leave you with

many other alternatives, does it?' Gideon asked her softly.

'I will repay you... I just need more time,' Courage protested.

'Which I'm not prepared to give you... No, my dear Courage, I fear you really have no option but to give in and——'

'Why are you doing this?' Courage whispered, white-faced. 'Why are you demeaning us both in this way? You can't possibly really want me, and I certainly don't want you...'

'No? That wasn't what you said the other night,' he reminded her mockingly. 'Then, you said——'

'No... No...' Trembling in despair, Courage clapped her hands over her ears. 'Please don't do this,' she begged him as his hand went back to his shirt, flicking open the last few buttons before reaching for the fastening on his trousers. 'I can't...'

'You can't, what?' Gideon taunted her. 'You can't accept me as your lover? But you already have, re-member...? And you seemed happy enough to do so. More than happy... In fact, as I remember it...'

Frantically Courage looked past him towards the bedroom door.

'Run if you like,' Gideon told her carelessly. 'But if you do, don't forget what I said, Courage... One way or another I intend to obtain repayment of the money you owe me. Either through the use of your extremely desirable and experienced little body or through your grandmother... The choice is yours.'

Choice—what choice? Courage wanted to demand, but she couldn't trust herself to speak without com-pletely breaking down. Was this really the man she had believed she had loved? Now she hated him—loathed him. The very thought of him coming anywhere near her, never mind touching her, filled her with furious rage and loathing.

'Well? Made your mind up yet?' Gideon asked her softly.

Courage glared at him; she wasn't going to plead with him, to beg and further humiliate herself for his enjoyment, but, despite knowing how much he would enjoy watching her demean herself in such a way, she still couldn't stop herself denying shakily, 'I *don't* want to go to bed with you—to make love with you...'

'We won't *be* making love. We'll be having sex,' Gideon told her curtly.

Having sex. Courage could feel the shudder threatening to grip her body and completely destroy her composure.

'Now,' she heard Gideon saying softly, as she turned away from him to conceal her expression from him. 'Are you going to get undressed or do you want me to do it for you...?'

Courage had had enough. She had only two options open to her now: either she gave in to her fear and let Gideon see how much he was hurting her—let him guess the love she had felt for him which he was now destroying—or she fought what she was feeling and let him see that while she could do nothing to stop him using her body he would never be able to humiliate or hurt her emotionally or mentally.

Turning round to face him, she drew herself up to her full height and told him dispassionately, 'I really don't see that there's any need for me to undress. I can have sex with you just as easily with my clothes on as with them off and, to be honest, as far as I'm concerned the less physical contact I have to have with you the better. To me, skin to skin contact is like kissing...something special and intimate that should only be shared with a lover...'

It was the hardest speech she had ever had to make, and in many ways the most shaming and hurtful, implying as it did that she had the experience to back up her clinically detached statements, but at least she had the satisfaction of seeing in Gideon's eyes—before he quickly hid his expression from her—that she had caught him off-guard, that he had not expected that kind of retaliation from her.

'I see. Tell me, then, how do you explain away your behaviour the other night? As I recall, you were far from averse on that occasion—not just to the removal of your clothes, but to... er... "skin to skin contact" as well. In fact, unless my memory is playing tricks on me, I seem to remember hearing you whisper certain hot little pleas in my ear concerning your need to have even more intimate "skin to skin contact" with my body.'

Courage could feel her face turning red and then white.

'That... that was different,' she whispered.

'Why, because then you believed I didn't know who you were...? Because then you thought you were free to play your clever little game of eager excitement and faked innocence...? Right down to that extremely effective clenching of your muscles, just at the right moment to fake virginity... Most impressive... Although I doubt that many men these days would expect to find a woman of your age still intact. However, I suppose there are one or two about still gullible and vulnerable enough to fall for that kind of trick.'

'It wasn't a——' Abruptly Courage stopped.

'Very sensible,' Gideon approved mockingly. 'Anyway, why bother lying anyway? You probably weren't even a virgin all those years ago, and if you had been...'

'You wouldn't have wanted to know,' Courage finished bitterly for him. 'Yes. I do realise that. After all, it wasn't me you expected in the first place, was it? It was my stepsister...'

'She'd been giving me come-on signs for weeks...' Gideon gave a careless shrug. 'Sex was still something of a novelty to me in those days, and I didn't——'

'Care who you had it with?' Courage interrupted acidly. 'So what's changed?'

She turned away from him as she spoke, and then froze in shock as he moved so quickly that she didn't even realise what was happening until he was holding her, imprisoning her, with one arm pinning her against his body, long, lean fingers digging painfully into her waist, while the other hand curled round her throat, forcing her face up towards his own.

'Oh, I care,' he told her throatily. 'In fact, I care so much that in anticipation of the pleasure I'm going to have with you I've been celibate for what is beginning to feel like one hell of a long time...'

Despite the way her body was starting to shake, from somewhere Courage found the strength to tell him breathlessly, 'That's not true... The other night...'

'The other night was nothing...' Gideon told her silkily. 'I hope you've had plenty of sleep while I've been away, because I promise you, you aren't going to get much tonight.'

To her shock, Courage felt her whole body jerk in physical response to what he was saying, as though he had somehow already touched it in the most intimate and physically compelling way.

She didn't believe it. How *could* her body be physically responsive to him when mentally and emotionally she now loathed him... hated him?

But she could see from Gideon's expression that he had already registered that give-away reaction of her body, and that he was responding to it.

Outside, the thunder which had been steadily rumbling ominously closer suddenly burst into a shattering explosion of noise, quickly followed by an intense flash of lightning, distracting Courage's attention away from Gideon, her body suddenly stiffening as she felt the warmth of his hands on the bare skin of her back beneath her top.

'You can always change your mind,' Gideon taunted her as he unclipped her bra and then unfastened the buttons securing her top. 'Just say the word and I'll collect repayment of your debt from your grandmother instead...'

'You know I can't let you do that,' Courage told him. You're not a man—you're not even human,' she spat out at him when he stopped her instinctive movement to cross her arms over her bare breasts as he removed her clothes.

She wasn't going to give him the satisfaction of fighting physically with him, of panicking and giving him an excuse to manhandle and maul her even more than he was doing now, and besides...

Her face flushed and she refused to give in to the temptation of looking down at her body. She didn't really need to confirm her fear that her nipples—reacting, surely, to the brush of warm air against their nakedness and certainly not to the fact that Gideon was looking at them—had suddenly hardened, thrusting erotically swollen peaks into full view.

She wasn't going to fall into the trap of remembering how it had felt when Gideon had touched them, kissed them, drawn them into his mouth and suckled on them until she had cried out against the almost unbearable pangs of pleasure he was giving her. Things had been different then; *she* had been different.

'Amazing,' she heard Gideon drawl. 'How do you *do* that, I wonder? A professional secret, no doubt.'

Beneath the gritty cynicism in his voice Courage could hear a sensual roughness that alarmed her more than his cynicism ever could.

It warned her that he was aroused, that he had not been lying earlier when he had told her he wanted her.

'Are you going to take off the rest, or shall I do it for you?' she heard him asking her.

'I'm not undressing for you,' Courage responded angrily. 'And if you——'

'No...? Then just remember that this was your choice,' Gideon warned her, cutting through her speech and grabbing hold of her, picking her up before she could stop him and carrying her the short distance to the waiting bed.

Outside, the sky was almost black now, the rain hissing against the windows, the air inside the room almost stiflingly unbreathable.

Courage could feel the sweat breaking out on her skin, even while she was shivering with shock and dread.

'It's too late to change your mind now,' Gideon mocked her as he lowered her to the bed without letting her go.

She stared fixedly over his shoulder, determinedly ignoring the proximity of his half-clad body, refusing to acknowledge the effect the hot, male scent of his skin was having on her memory patterns, on her female responsiveness, clamping down tightly on every muscle within her body—but most especially that part of her that refused to listen to what her brain and her emotions were trying to tell it; that part of her which wantonly acknowledged only that the sexuality of the man holding her was erotically exciting to it, that it recognised him, wanted him.

'Now, let's get rid of these, shall we?' she heard Gideon saying softly as his fingers curled round the waistline of her elasticated leggings.

His face was on a level with her own as he looked mockingly down into her eyes, enjoying the angry flame of fury that burned there.

There was nothing she could do to stop him, Courage knew... Nothing dignified, that was. And if she did try to fight him, what chance did she have of succeeding?

Her glance slid betrayingly to his body—the breadth and depth of his chest, with its hard male muscles. Both her arms together were scarcely as thick as one of his, and as for the hands now inexorably tugging her leggings down... If Gideon had wished them to do so they could have gripped her waist so painfully hard that they would have crushed her vulnerable flesh.

She drew a shaky breath and closed her eyes against the demanding rush of tears that threatened to flood them.

The top of Gideon's head was just beneath her chin now; she could feel the soft brush of his hair, the warmth of his breath.

She could feel, as well, the touch of his knuckles against her hips as he continued to remove her leggings. Despairingly she wished bitterly that the whole thing was over, that he would hurry up and get it over instead of torturing her like this. But then he was enjoying her pain, her fear... her humiliation. Just as he'd told her he intended to do.

She shivered as she felt the warmth of his breath in the valley between her breasts, and then froze as she felt his mouth slowly caressing the soft swell of one breast.

Somehow she had not expected this. Somehow she had assumed that his possession of her would merely involve a detached conjoining of their bodies. That he might want to indulge in love-play... to caress her... to arouse her as he had done before, was something that had never occurred to her.

Frantically she tried to push his head away, but it was too late. His mouth was already caressing her nipple.

The fate of her leggings was forgotten as Courage fought not to give in to the physical compulsion that flooded her. The urge to curl her fingers into his hair and hold his head against her body was strong, so much stronger this time than it had been that first time... Because now her body knew the pleasure that Gideon could give it.

Courage's face burned with humiliated shame. How could her body still want him like this—still ache so wantonly for him? Tears burned her eyes behind her closed eyelids.

How triumphant Gideon would be if he knew what he was doing to her... how much she wanted him.

His mouth moved on to her other breast, and Courage had to dig her nails into the bed beneath her to stop herself from reaching up to him. Her whole body was rigid with the muscle tension she had imposed on it in an attempt to prevent herself from betraying what she was feeling.

But beneath her locked muscles she could feel the urgency of its rebellion, its hungry need to soften and move in seductive incitement, its heated, quivering desire to feel Gideon moving within it.

She could feel the warmth of his breath against her stomach now, the tip of his tongue drawing tormenting circles around her navel.

With a shock of horror, Courage realised that he intended to follow the removal of her clothes with the mocking exploration of his mouth and tongue. Too late now to wish that she had never challenged him, that she had simply removed her clothes herself.

She should have known how much delight he would take in punishing her for her defiance. After all, he already knew just what the intimacy of the kind of caresses he was inflicting on her now would do to her self-control, and he must know, as well, how much she would despise herself for her physical reaction to him.

It was different for a man, of course, she acknowledged bitterly. A man need not feel any sense of shame or self-contempt, need not despise himself for being physically aroused by a woman he did not love and who did not love him. Certainly Gideon had already made it more than plain that he felt not the least little bit of discomfort in acknowledging his desire for her.

His hands were on the top of her thighs now...her naked thighs. Her muscles, unable to bear the strains he was imposing on them, started to tremble—only the finest of internal tremors at first, and then, as her control slipped, open shivers of frantic movement.

'So many clever little tricks,' she heard Gideon exclaiming in marvelling tones as he opened his hands, his fingers cool and hard, palms flat down on her trembling thighs, measuring their jerky, uncontrollable self-betrayal.

'But I've already told you,' he continued, his voice hardening, 'there's no point in you faking inexperienced apprehension. So those delightfully erotic little shivers of mock-uncontrollable arousal are completely wasted on me.'

The taunting cruelty of his words snapped the final thread of Courage's self-control.

'I'm not faking anything,' she told him furiously, angry tears shimmering in her eyes as she glared bitterly into the gaze he had lifted to meet hers. 'And for your information, I wouldn't even *know* how to fake it. I don't even know——' She stopped abruptly, appalled to hear what she was saying.

'I just want to get this whole thing over and done with,' she mumbled, unable to bear looking at him any more. 'I just want it over. Do you understand?' she repeated shakily, her hands balled into two small, tight fists at her sides.

'Oh, yes. I understand,' she heard Gideon saying, with a soft emphasis that made fresh alarm flare inside her. 'I understand very well indeed.

'So what you are saying is that you don't want me to touch you like this?' he asked her throatily as his fingertips caressed her still-trembling thigh, causing Courage to catch her breath audibly and, equally betrayingly, to try and move her body out of his reach.

'Or like this...?' Gideon continued smoothly, with even more throaty emphasis. He watched her frantic attempts to control her body while he stroked even closer to the intimate heart of her body.

'Or like this...?' This time his voice was slightly muffled as he bent his head and placed his mouth to her body, which reacted as helplessly as though a bolt of lightning from the storm outside had jolted right through it.

Her panicky, 'No—no, don't...' was ignored as easily as the movement of her hands as she tried to dislodge Gideon.

She couldn't bear to look down to where she knew his dark head lay, between her now openly trembling thighs.

His touch as his fingers parted the protective outer lips to her sex was as gentle and careful as though they genuinely were lovers. He used no force or aggression. But then he didn't need to, Courage acknowledged in miserable humiliation. She would almost have preferred it if he had had to. Anything would have been preferable to knowing how much her body wanted the intimacy of the caresses he was offering it.

How eagerly it swelled for the sensual invasion of his tongue, the hot, erotic possession of his mouth. The frantic cries of denial she was making might have been authorised and legitimised by her brain, but her body was openly and wantonly denying every one of them, aligning itself to Gideon, laughing at her, betraying her.

Panic seized her as she fought to control the drugging pleasure he was giving her body and realised that she couldn't—that the need and longing he was arousing within her were too strong for her to subdue. That shamingly, while her shocked, bruised emotions and brain recoiled from the unbearable intimacy of the caresses he was giving her, her body was responding to them with an intensity that flagrantly ignored her demands to it not to do so.

'Oh, yes, you certainly want to get it over and done with,' Gideon taunted her as he pulled away slightly and then began feathering tormentingly brief kisses against the quivering flesh of her stomach.

Tears stung Courage's eyes. How he must hate her to want to do this to her. But, as much as he hated and loathed her, she knew that his hatred and loathing could not possibly come anywhere near matching her own. Her body's betrayal of her was the most frightening thing she had ever experienced, and the most humiliating.

There was just enough light left now for Courage to see that Gideon's body glistened slightly with sweat, and that the hand he stretched out to smooth from her hip to her breast trembled slightly as it touched her—but not as much as she trembled as he bent his head and kissed the hollow between her breasts, and then the breast itself.

She stiffened and tried to push him away as she felt the brush of his thighs against her body.

'It's too late now to feign reluctance,' she heard him telling her thickly. 'You want me and you know it.'

'No.' Courage denied, summoning the last of her strength to defy him. 'My body wants you...my flesh. But that's only because it doesn't have the capability, the ability to recognise what you really are. It only knows that you can arouse it. But my body is not the whole of me, Gideon... It isn't my mind, my consciousness...the real essence of me...my heart and my emotions... They don't want you, because they know you for what you really are...'

She cried out as she felt him seize hold of her arms, smothering her defiant words with the hot, hard pressure of his mouth, her whole body shuddering as he moved against it and she felt the first powerful surge of his body within her own.

This wasn't making love, she acknowledged bitterly as she fought to suppress the tears she could feel threatening to fall. It wasn't even sex. It was a battle...war... A fierce, silent struggle in which each of them fought to destroy the other, to drive the other to a point where they would lose control and fall helplessly into the empty, agonisingly lonely space that lay beyond the edge of that final precipice.

In virtually the same instant as her body felt the pleasure of that exquisite sensation of total release, her emotions, her heart, her soul were plunged into a pit of the darkest despair.

This should not be happening. Her body should not be able to experience so much pleasure, so much fulfillment, with a man she must not love... A man who did not love her.

As her body trembled in the aftermath of physical release, the perspiration cooling on her over-heated skin, the ache of emotional pain within her was more than she could bear.

Behind her slightly closed eyelids she could feel the hot burn of the tears she ached to cry. Gideon was lying close to her, still holding her in his arms for some unfathomable reason—probably so that he could torment her still further by mocking her for her response to him.

She flinched openly as he moved closer to her, and then stiffened in disbelief as she felt his lips moving gently against her skin, her throat, her jaw, the corners of her now tightly closed eyes. His breath was warm and disconcertingly unsteady as it touched her flesh—surely a sign which from any other man a woman—even one as inexperienced as herself—might logically interpret as an indication of emotional arousal equally as strong as the physical arousal he had so recently demonstrated. That simply couldn't be the case where Gideon was concerned, though—not with her. Not when he had been at such pains to make his contempt and dislike of her so very, very clear.

Her throat ached as she felt his fingertips touch her mouth in gentle exploration, tracing its outline almost lingeringly. She heard him draw in his breath, and then it was the turn of her own breathing to betray her as she felt his lips brush hers, slowly and carefully.

Wasn't this what every woman longed for—a lover who would continue to show her physical affection and emotional tenderness even after his desire for her had been satiated? She certainly had dreamed of it, but now even the sanctity of that special female ideal had been destroyed for her by Gideon's cruel pretence.

If she and Gideon *had* really been lovers—if he *had* shared the love and need she felt for him—these moments held fast in his arms while he covered her face in gentle kisses and placed her hand against the damp warmth of his body, just where his heart was still thudding so heavily, would surely have been some of the most precious they would ever share, the most treasured in her memories. As it was...

'Don't...' Courage begged him, her denial scraping painfully against her tense, dry throat, as she tried to pull her hand away. 'What is it...? What more do you want?' she cried out emotionally when he refused to let her go. 'You've done what you wanted. Had what you wanted!'

And in doing so had completely destroyed her dreams, her deepest held beliefs about herself and her sexuality and the man with whom she would share it.

'Not yet, I haven't,' Gideon contradicted her flatly. 'Not by a long chalk. This is just the beginning—the first instalment on a debt on which the interest is still running—and at compound rates...

'Like I've already said, there's something about you that makes me ache...*itch* in a way that demands immediate and intense satisfaction...'

In the early hours of the morning, when Courage cried out in her sleep, tormented even in her dreams by the contrast between the fiction of her idealised imaginings of the man who would be her one and only lover and the reality, although neither she herself nor Gideon was aware of it the arm he had wrapped possessively around her body tightened, drawing her into the warmth of his body, and a deep frown drew his eyebrows together, as though somehow in his own sleep he was aware of her misery, her tears, and sought to comfort her.

CHAPTER ELEVEN

'COURAGE, you've got a visitor.'

Wan-faced, Courage paused, turning round to acknowledge Jenny's comment as she made her way across the hall en route for her office.

She had just returned from visiting her grandmother, who was now out of bed and apparently thoroughly enjoying her period of recuperation. The specialist was certainly extremely pleased with her progress, according to what he had told Courage.

Everyone, it seemed to Courage, was happy. Everyone bar herself.

She knew that in normal circumstances her grandmother would have been the first to notice how pale and ill she was looking, and to demand to know what was wrong.

It was just as well she had *not* noticed. How could she have told her the truth? What would she have said to her? Courage wondered mirthlessly. That she was having to satisfy Gideon's sexual needs as a means of repaying the money she had borrowed from him to pay for the operation?

Wasn't it illegal for a woman to sell her body to a man for money? Tears burned hotly behind her eyes. Quickly she blinked them away. She was proud of the fact that she hadn't cried once—not once since that dreadful night when Gideon had confronted her with his diabolical demands.

'He said he was a friend so I took him over to your apartment,' Jenny was explaining.

A friend? Courage frowned.

'I——'

'Oh, and Gideon rang. He said to tell you that he was going to be delayed in London with Princess Maryam, but that that didn't change his plans for tonight. He said you would know what he meant.'

Courage couldn't help it. She could feel her face starting to sting with hot colour.

Gideon had laughed at her for her insistence on returning to her own bed every night—or rather, every morning.

Shockingly, to her at least, it seemed that Gideon wasn't content with taking her to bed each and every single night he was at home; his desire for her was still just as strong in the early hours of the day, leaving Courage with no alternative but to remain in his bed until he deigned to let her go.

'Who is it you are trying to deceive with this pathetic insistence on returning to your own bed?' he had demanded one morning as she had crept, still trembling, from his bed to snatch up her discarded clothes while he watched her tauntingly.

'I don't want Jenny to know that... I don't want her to know what's happening,' she had told him.

But it wasn't just at night that he had insisted on calling in her 'repayments' on her debt. The other day he had returned early from a business trip to Cornwall, walking into his office while she was placing some papers on his desk.

When he had seen her he had turned back and with deliberation locked the door and started to remove his jacket, all the time maintaining an eye-contact with her which had made her feel like a terrified, mesmerised rabbit.

The swiftness and intensity with which he had then possessed her should have been something she recoiled from in disdain and disgust; something which surely she should have immediately and totally expunged from her memory. Instead...

'Your visitor...' Jenny reminded her.

Tiredly Courage turned round. She certainly wasn't expecting a visit from anyone. It was probably someone who knew her grandmother and wanted to know how she was.

However, as she crossed the gravel courtyard in front of the stable-block and saw the car parked there with its Swiss plates, she realised that she had been wrong.

Jenny had used the pass-keys Courage had left with her to let Courage's visitor into her apartment, and as Courage herself entered the sitting-room a man got up from the sofa where he had been seated reading a newspaper and came towards her, smiling affectionately as he held out his arms to her.

'Gunther,' Courage exclaimed shakily as she returned her ex-employer's warm smile and moved into them to be firmly embraced. 'What are you *doing* here? How did you——?'

'I'm here on a family-cum-business visit to my grandmother's English relations. My father insisted that I call on you to see if I could persuade you to change your mind and return to work for us.'

'I can't, I'm afraid,' Courage told him.

Gunther was the eldest son of the Swiss family who owned the chain of hotels Courage had worked for; he had never made any secret of his fondness for her. They had gone out on a couple of dates together when Courage had first gone to work for his family, but once she had recognised how much more serious his feelings were than her own Courage had quickly, gently made it clear to him that, much as she liked him, liking was all she did feel for him.

They had remained good friends and Gunther had been the first person Courage had confided in when she had decided to give up her career and return home to her grandmother.

'Your grandmother isn't any better?' Gunther asked her frowningly now. 'I thought you said that after a rest . . .'

'Her condition turned out to be more serious than even the specialist realised,' Courage told him. 'Gran had to have a very serious operation. She came through it very well but I doubt that she will be able to live alone for quite some time—if at all... I'd love to come back, Gunther, but I'm afraid it just isn't possible.'

'I rather suspected that would be your answer,' Gunther told her wryly. 'You're very sorely missed, you know, and if at any time in the future you should change your mind...'

Courage was already walking him to the door.

'I couldn't expect you to hold open my job indefinitely,' she told him, shaking her head a little as they both stepped out into the late afternoon sunshine.

'It isn't just a job that would be waiting for you if you came back to us,' Gunther told her softly as they walked towards his car.

Out of the corner of her eye Courage saw Gideon's car sweep round the corner and come to an abrupt halt, sending up a flurry of gravel.

She stiffened immediately, tension running through her body like a fine electric current. Gunther frowned as he looked across at where Gideon was getting out of his car.

'Have dinner with me tonight,' he urged her. 'We could——'

Quickly Courage interrupted him.

'I can't... I... I... It was kind of you to come and see me, Gunther, and to... to offer me my job back. But...'

She could feel her throat starting to close up. How could she even begin to explain to this patient, gentle, *decent* man just how much her life had changed? Just how much *she* had changed. If he knew the truth about her... about what she was... what she'd become...

She could feel his concern as he reached out and touched her arm, his touch respectful and hesitant.

'Courage...'

Courage could feel the panic building up inside her as she saw Gideon walking towards them, his mouth compressed in anger.

'Gunther... I have to go back to work... I...'

It hurt so much being reminded of the life which had once been hers. All that was gone now, and she was chained here to a man who loathed her as much as she...

As much as she, what? she asked herself shakily as Gunther obeyed her command and headed for his car.

'Who was that?' Gideon demanded peremptorily as he reached Courage's side, just as Gunther started to drive away.

'No one... An old friend...' Courage told him, her face suddenly flushing as she followed the line of Gideon's narrowed gaze towards the open door to her apartment.

'How long was he here for?' Gideon demanded.

Courage's head was beginning to ache. She felt sick and dizzy. She had had nothing to eat since this morning, and then only half a slice of toast. She felt so tired at the moment that somehow eating just seemed to be another unpleasant chore she had to get through.

'I...I don't know... An hour...maybe more...'

She had no idea what time Gunther had arrived, and now she realised guiltily that she hadn't even offered him a drink.

'An hour...maybe more...' Gideon repeated silkily. 'An hour, maybe more, of *my* time, that would be, I take it? Time for which I *pay* you. Time which you now *owe* me.' His hand shot out, his fingers digging painfully into the flesh of her upper arm as he held her fast. 'So that's another debt you owe me. Another——''

He broke off, frowning, as his car-phone suddenly started to ring.

For a moment Courage thought that he was going to ignore it...that he might actually drag her up the stairs to her apartment and exact payment for the time he believed she had stolen from him right there and then. But to her relief, he released her instead, and strode back to his car.

Courage didn't wait for him to continue tormenting her. She fled to the sanctuary of her apartment, locking and bolting the door behind her before going into her bedroom and collapsing on to the bed.

She couldn't go on like this. It was destroying her— *Gideon* was destroying her—and what made it worse was the fact that no matter how much she loathed and hated what he was doing to her with her mind and her emotions...how much she told herself she hated him physically...the moment he touched her her body responded to him as though...as though...as though it loved and adored him, craved and ached for him, yearned for him, needed him, loved him totally and completely and forever.

With a low moan she buried her face in her pillow, trying to stifle the dry sobs that racked her body. Her head ached so much, her eyes felt dry and sore, her throat... She was shivering, even though in reality she felt too hot, and she was so tired that she felt she could never get enough sleep—she had neither eaten nor slept properly for days.

She had known without Jenny telling her so that she had lost weight, that she looked not just fine-boned now but actually gaunt. She had felt the measuring quality of Gideon's touch only the other night, as though he was silently assessing the meagreness of her flesh.

Men didn't like thin, bony women, did they...? Maybe her loss of weight would turn Gideon off her... Maybe. She could hear Gideon hammering on the apartment door, calling her name. Gritting her teeth, she pulled the pillow down tightly around her ears. She knew what would happen if she got up and let him in.

A tiny tell-tale ache, a small, sickening surge of anticipatory pleasure made her tense her body in shamed self-disgust. How *could* she feel like this...? *Want* him so much when...?

Her head was throbbing so painfully that she felt as ough it might burst. There were some painkillers in e bathroom cabinet...

Shakily she got up and went to get them. The knocking ad ceased now. Gideon had obviously gone away to ide his time; he would no doubt punish her for her subordination later.

A deep shudder galvanised her body. She took two of e tablets and then another two, grimacing as she ashed down the bitter taste with some water.

She knew she really ought to have something to eat, shower and wash away the signs of her tears and eariness and get back to work. That was the one good ing about her present state of nervous tension—her ability to sleep meant that her work was always com-letely up to date, despite the time she had off to visit er gran. She was far from owing Gideon time. If the uth were known, *he* was the one who was in debt to er.

Muzzily she made her way back to her bedroom, half rawling, half collapsing on to her bed as the double ose of the strong painkillers took effect on her empty omach.

ourage cried out in her sleep, tormented by nightmare emories from the past. Images of her stepfather and er stepsister and the fear and pain they had brought to her life. Images of the first time she had met Gideon, e sweet, savage shock of being awakened by him to er own sensuality. Images of Gideon as he was now.

As she cried out in pain, the tears pouring down her ace, she felt someone take hold of her and shake her, ringing her out of her tortured sleep. Instinctively she tiffened her body as she started to wake up, already nticipating whose hand it was that had brought her back reality. Only when she opened her eyes it wasn't ideon who was waking her, asking her what was wrong, ut Jenny.

'Jenny...' Confused and shaken, Courage pressed h
hands to her hot face. 'What time is it...? What a
you doing here...?'

'It's four o'clock in the morning,' Jenny told h
quietly. 'I heard you crying, and you sounded so di
tressed that I decided to use the pass-keys you'd left wi
me and come in to see what was wrong...'

'I was having a bad dream...' Courage told her. 'I...

'A bad dream?' Jenny gave her a compassionate loo
'This isn't the first time I've heard you crying in th
night, Courage. Something's obviously very wrong. Th
man who came to see you today—was he——?'

'No. No...this has nothing to do with Gunther
Courage assured her quickly. No matter how much sh
wanted to keep her shame and degradation private, sh
couldn't allow Gunther to be blamed for her misery.

'But it is a man, isn't it?' Jenny guessed, refusing t
give up. 'And if it isn't your visitor, then it mus
be——'

'Please, Jenny, don't...' Courage begged her.
can't...' To her distress Courage felt fresh tears floodin
from her eyes, her voice suspended by emotion.

'I may not be young any more, but I do know how
feels to love a man who... Have you thought that
might be in your best interests to find another job?' sh
counselled gently. 'To leave while...'

'Leave?' Courage cried out in anguish. 'If only
could.' And then she bit her lip as she realised she ha
said too much.

'My daughter is several years older than you, but
would break my heart if I thought she was going throug
the kind of emotional trauma I know you're sufferin
without anyone to help her. Please let me help you
Courage. I promise you that what you say to me won'
go any further.'

Tears trickled silently down Courage's face as sh
fought the temptation to unburden herself, and lost
Slowly, haltingly, she started to tell Jenny what had hap

ened—all of it—right from the first night she had met
Gideon.

Several times she had to stop when her emotions overwhelmed her, and gulp gratefully at the hot tea Jenny
had made for them both.

'He's actually blackmailing you into having sex with
him?' Jenny repeated flatly. 'That's diabolical, de-
moniacal, inhuman... It's...it's virtually a form of
rape...'

Courage hung her head.

'No...no it isn't that,' she told Jenny quietly. 'That's
what makes the whole thing so...so...so hurtful. I want
him, you see, Jenny. Or rather, my body does...' Her
mouth twisted bitterly. 'I know with my mind that he
isn't the lover I so foolishly dreamed of, but my body
refuses to acknowledge that fact...'

'You mustn't pillory yourself,' Jenny told her fiercely.
You've done nothing wrong. Nothing to deserve such
cruelty and——'

'I caused him to lose his job,' Courage reminded her
onelessly, 'and——'

'You were a girl...a child, almost, and from what
you've told me... How much money do you owe him,
Courage?'

'I'm not sure. The original loan was for ten thousand
pounds, but then there's the interest... I...'

'I'll lend you twelve thousand, that ought to cover it,'
Jenny told her briskly. 'I'll give you a cheque in the
morning. You can pay it straight into your bank and
draw against it to pay off Gideon.'

'*You'll* lend me the m-money...?' Courage stammered. 'But...'

'But, what...? No buts, Courage. My late husband
left me very comfortably provided for. I don't *have* to
work to support myself—I do it as a means of keeping
myself occupied, of not becoming a burden on my
children. I'm too old to want to find another man, form
another relationship, and too young to settle for re-

tirement. I *need* to work, to give my life a sense of purpose, but I don't, in all honesty, need the money...

'I...I don't know how I'm going to pay you back. won't have a job...'

'That will make two of us,' Jenny told her grimly 'Because I certainly shan't be staying on here now Couldn't you go back to your old job?'

'Yes,' Courage admitted. 'That was why Gunther, m visitor, came to see me...to ask me to go back... Bu I can't... Gran is going to need someone to look afte her once she comes home and——'

'I could do that.'

Courage looked uncertainly at the older woman.

'I couldn't expect you to do that. No... It's very kin of you, Jenny, but I can't... I can't let you lend me suc a large sum of money.'

'You mean, you'd rather go on owing it to Gideon?

'No, no of course I wouldn't,' Courage denied hotly 'Are you... are you really sure... ?'

'I'm really sure,' Jenny confirmed quietly, reaching out and taking Courage in her arms and giving her quick hug. 'Men can be so stupid... I've only know you a matter of weeks, but it's patently obvious to m that you could never be the kind of woman Gideon seem to assume. There is one thing, though.' She paused an looked thoughtfully at Courage. 'You say that he hate you, even though physically he desires you?'

'That's what he's always telling me,' Courage agreed shivering.

'Hatred and love can sometimes be so closely en twined that it's hard to tell them apart,' Jenny told her

'Yes,' Courage agreed bitterly. '*His* hatred and *m* love. Are you really sure about this, Jenny, about lendin me the money, I mean?'

'Positive,' Jenny confirmed firmly.

'Where is... where is Gideon, by the way?' Courag asked her suddenly, remembering his angry hammerin on her door earlier in the evening.

'In London. He's gone to see the Princess,' Jenny told her, watching her compassionately as the colour drained from her face, leaving it betraying what she was feeling.

'I always thought that when I loved a man it would be...that he would feel the same way; that we would have mutual respect for one another, and that...' Courage bit her lip, shaking her head as her emotions overwhelmed her.

'Can I see you for a moment, please, Gideon?'

Courage tensed herself ready for a refusal as Gideon frowned forbiddingly down at her. He had returned from London about an hour ago and she had been sitting dry-mouthed in her own office ever since, her stomach churning in anticipation of the moment when she would hand him the cheque to repay her loan.

She knew she ought to be feeling triumphant and relieved, but instead...

'What now? Can't it wait until later...until tonight...?'

Courage flushed brilliantly as his voice deepened with deliberate innuendo.

'No...no, I'm afraid it can't.' She told him. 'I...I want to give you this.'

Her hand trembled visibly as she slid the envelope on to his desk. She couldn't risk encouraging any kind of physical contact with him... She didn't dare.

She saw the way his frown deepened as he stared at the envelope before picking it up and opening it.

Courage knew that she was holding her breath. She desperately wanted to turn and run, but she refused to give in to such a cowardly temptation.

'I see... And where exactly did you get this?'

The carefully measured ice-cold words made Courage feel sick with apprehension. She knew him so well now—his moods, the controlled calm that preceded his anger.

'A...a friend gave it to me...' Not for anything was she going to betray Jenny's part in what had happened—ever. Even if Jenny *had* insisted that she was going to hand in her notice.

'A *friend* ... The same *friend* who I saw you bidding such a fond farewell to yesterday afternoon, no doubt. What did you do for him, Courage? What did you promise him in return for this? Unlimited access to your body...every kind of sexual favour and delight he might want...? And was it *just* a promise you gave him, or has he already had a foretaste of what kind of payment he's going to get? Perhaps he even already knows...

'Does he, Courage? Is that why he came here looking for you, because he knows just how good you are in bed? Just how you can drive a man insane with desire and lust? Just how you can incite him to want to possess you over and over again...? Is that it, Courage... Is *that* why he came here looking for you?

'Did he take you while you still had the scent of my possession—my sex—on your body? Did he——?'

'Stop it. Stop it!' Courage couldn't stand any more. Tears of rage and humiliation poured down her face. 'I hate you. I hate you—do you hear...? And I'm leaving here right now and there's nothing you can do to stop me... nothing.'

'Oh, no?'

While Courage watched, her heart pounding frantically in a mixture of anger and pain, he tore up the cheque she had just given him.

'You still owe me...' he told her silkily. 'And there's no way I'm letting you go away.

'How did he kiss you, Courage?' he demanded thickly as he reached for her, covering her mouth in a fiercely punishing kiss. 'Was it like this...? How did he touch you? What did you do for him to get him to part with that money? What...?'

His hand was already on her breast, and to her disgust Courage could feel her body starting to respond to his touch.

'Nothing. There was nothing,' she protested frantically.

'You're lying,' Gideon contradicted her flatly.

'No, she's not... I loaned her the money.'

Neither of them had heard the door open, or even seen Jenny come into the room.

'I loaned her the money after she broke down and told me how you'd treated her... blackmailed her. Go and pack your things, Courage,' Jenny told her quietly, before she turned back to Gideon and said coldly, 'In my view you should be imprisoned and disgraced for what you've done to Courage. But I know she's far too soft-hearted to share that opinion. You're a bully and a sadist, and even worse you're apparently incapable of compassion or understanding...'

Courage fled without waiting to hear any more.

Gideon's accusations and comments had left her feeling degraded and physically sick, and she knew that they would haunt her for the rest of her life.

As she packed her clothes haphazardly into her cases she acknowledged that she was lucky to have Gran's cottage to go to. She could stay there until Gran came home and then decide what to do about her future.

Right now she needed time—time to come to terms with what had happened and with herself, her own emotions, her self-betrayal.

Courage frowned as she studied her bank statement. It worried her that Gideon had still not cleared the cheque she had left on his desk to replace the one he had torn up, even though it was now almost a fortnight since she had left.

In another three weeks her grandmother would be coming home and Jenny, who was spending a couple of weeks visiting her daughter, had repeatedly assured Courage that she was more than happy to move in with her grandmother and keep an eye on her until the specialist pronounced her well enough to live alone again.

All she had to do now was telephone her old employers and tell them that she was free to come back to work for them and she could then draw a line under the past and write off everything that had happened since Gideon had come back into her life.

Pain darkened her eyes. If only things were so easy. She still woke up in the night with Gideon's name on her lips and her face wet with tears.

What was *wrong* with her? She knew what kind of man he was...how lucky she had been to escape from him.

'During the day I'm all right—sort of,' she had told Jenny shakily. 'It's at night, when I remember...when I dream... It's as though a part of me still refuses to accept the way he really is...still clings to the feelings I had for him when I was sixteen.'

'Loving someone, especially when it's the wrong someone, isn't easy to get over,' Jenny had comforted her. 'It takes time, Courage. After all, you've spent years clinging to him as your ideal—your perfect lover. When my husband died I was so very angry... With myself because I hadn't realised how ill he was... With the hospital because they hadn't been able to save him, and with him too, for dying and leaving me alone...unprepared... My doctor sent me to a counsellor, who told me to try writing down exactly how I felt. How I'd felt before he died and then afterwards... Although I didn't think it would, it did actually help. You could always try doing the same thing.'

Writing it down, reliving all that pain—what purpose would it serve? Courage had asked herself. But still she had followed Jenny's advice...was still following it— faithfully recording everything that had happened in the hours leading up to that first cataclysmic meeting with Gideon, when she hadn't known who he was...the trauma which had followed...her immature, un- awakened idealisation of him...her foolish belief that because he had slept with her it must mean he loved her...and the starkness of what had followed, with its disillusionment and pain.

It hadn't helped, though. All it had done was to make her dreams of him all the more intense, like her longing for him. Quickly she bit down on her lip.

The evenings were starting to draw in now. Summer was over and autumn had begun. The fields beyond the house were covered in mist in the mornings and the air had a sharp chill to it at night. It was only eight o'clock but already it was almost dark.

The evenings were the worst time for her. During the day she managed to keep busy, to keep her thoughts and her emotions at bay, but in the evening, with the knowledge that the night lay ahead of her...

Tonight, for some reason, she had decided to light a fire. Now it needed more logs, and she would have to go out to the outhouse to get them.

Picking up the log basket, she headed for the back door, leaving it open as she covered the short distance between it and the outhouse. It took nearly five minutes for her to fill the basket, which was then so heavy that she could barely carry it in.

Once she had reached the kitchen she put it down with a sigh of relief before going to close and lock the back door, grimacing as she saw the dust and grime on her hands.

She picked up the basket again, using her hip to push open the sitting-room door. Her view of the room was obstructed by the basket, so that she didn't realise until she had reached the fireplace and set it down that someone else was already in the room.

The shock made her body feel cold and heavy. 'Gideon,' she whispered in disbelief. 'What are...? How did you get in...? What are you doing here?'

'The door was open. I wanted to see you... I *had* to see you.'

He looked different—thinner... more tired... older, somehow.

'I'm not coming back. You... you can't make me...' she started to protest in panic, backing away from him, her hand held out defensively in front of her body as though to ward him off.

An expression that in another man might have been pain touched his eyes, fleetingly hardening his face.

'No. I can't make you,' he agreed heavily. 'Your grandmother tells me that she'll be coming home soon.'

'Not for another few weeks,' Courage told him automatically, before freezing and demanding anxiously, 'How do you know that? What have you said to her...? What have you done...?'

'I haven't done anything, and as for what I've said to her, it's more a matter of what she has said to me. It seems I owe you an apology, Courage. Several apologies, in fact. I had no idea... It never occurred to me... I hadn't realised how young you were, emotionally and sexually. You were so warm...so welcoming. So apparently knowing. I was wrong about you all those years ago,' he told her bleakly. 'Very wrong...'

Courage shivered. 'What have you been saying to her? What have you——'

'I simply asked her if she would mind talking to me about the past. She was very candid...very open... Especially in her denouncement of your stepfather. She seemed to think there was even a risk that he might——'

Courage listened, her lips dry with fear and shame, and a nauseous mixture in her stomach.

'I don't want to talk about it. It's over...finished... And...and nothing ever actually happened...'

'But you were afraid it might?' Gideon pressed her.

'I...I was afraid,' Courage admitted unable to say any more.

'And that was why you agreed to take your stepsister's place with me?'

'I... She... Yes. She was jealous of her father's attention towards me. I...I think she wanted to discredit me in his eyes... I don't think she ever had any intention of hurting you. Why are you bringing this up now?' she asked him shakily. 'I don't want to talk about it. It's over...finished...'

'Is it...? I don't think so. There's still——'

'There's still what?' Courage interrupted him frantically. 'Still the money I owe you? The loan...?'

'The loan is cancelled,' Gideon told her heavily. 'It no longer exists.'

For a moment Courage thought she must have misheard him.

'It's the least I can do,' Gideon continued distantly. 'Call it compensation, if you wish, for——'

'Compensation...' Courage stared at him, fury taking the place of her earlier fear. 'Compensation... Do you honestly think that money—that *anything* could *ever* compensate me for what you've done...for what you've made me do? For the way you've destroyed everything that I've ever believed in...everything that I've ever valued? Do you think money is going to stop me lying awake at night, filled with loathing and disgust for myself...? Do you think it is ever going to make me feel whole again...clean...? Make me believe that I can...give myself...share my life with a decent, caring man who loves me? A man who I can't, daren't let know what I've done. What kind of woman I really am...'

'And what kind of woman is that?' Gideon interrupted her quietly.

'What kind——?' Courage gave a bitter laugh. 'Surely *you* don't need to ask—*you* already know.'

Tears burned hotly in her eyes, blurring her vision, but even so she forced herself to raise her head and look straight at him.

'After all, you were the one who destroyed my illusions about myself, who made me see that no matter how much I might loathe and hate you with my mind, my body——' Courage heard her voice crack and knew that she couldn't go on.

'Your body responded to me...wanted me...as mine wanted you.'

'Everyone knows that it's perfectly acceptable for a *man* to experience lust. To——'

'Lust? My God, you are naïve. Lust doesn't make you cry out with longing for someone at night. It doesn't make you ache for them and yearn for them. It doesn't fill your every waking thought with them and drive you to the point of insanity through wanting them. Lust doesn't possess and obsess you to the point where nothing else, no one else matters... Lust doesn't fill you with blind, insane jealousy. It doesn't warp your thinking, and twist your guts into knots. Lust doesn't make you weep for the warmth of someone's arms, for the comfort of their body. It doesn't make you long to break down the barriers they've put around themselves and make them respond to your emotions... your needs... your desire. But love does!'

Courage had gone white as she listened to him cataloguing her emotions with such deadly accuracy that she felt as though he had witnessed every single one of them. All the time, when she had clung to the belief that at least he didn't know, couldn't know how she really felt about him, she had been wrong...

She clung shakily to the back of the chair as she stammered. 'How... how did you know that I... that I felt like that...?'

It must be much hotter in the room than she had realised, because all of a sudden his face looked unfamiliarly flushed.

'I didn't,' he told her roughly. 'Those weren't your emotions I was just describing, they were mine.'

Courage stared at him in total disbelief.

'You can't mean that,' she protested shakily. 'You can't really love me...'

'Why not? Because I hurt you... tried to demolish and destroy you? Love isn't always pure and innocent. It has its dark side too. I wanted you very badly that night, you know...'

'You didn't know me,' Courage protested. 'You thought I was Laney. It was her you were expecting. Her you wanted...'

Gideon shook his head.

'I was filling in time, that was all... Playing the same game I thought she was playing... Until I held you... touched you... kissed you—and then I knew.'

He stopped speaking abruptly, his body tensing.

'I dreamed of you that night,' he told her huskily, 'and for what felt like a lifetime of nights afterwards. In fact...' He frowned and paused. 'I've never stopped dreaming about you...not totally. Every time I thought I'd put the past behind me, pushed you out of my mind, my dreams, my memories, you'd come back again to haunt me. I dreamed about you the night before you came for your interview.'

'You wanted to hurt me...punish me...' Courage reminded him.

'I wanted to hurt and punish myself. To make myself realise just what you were. Only, it didn't work. The more I tried to rid myself of my feelings for you, the more enmeshed I became in them.

'You must have realised,' he told her harshly. 'When I touched you...held you...made love to you. You must have known...guessed...'

'You said it was just sex,' Courage told him huskily. 'You said——'

'You must have known,' Gideon insisted, overriding her disjointed speech.

'*You* didn't know that I was...that I hadn't...that there hadn't been anyone else,' Courage told him quietly.

Fresh tears blurred her eyes as she saw the way he was looking at her, the pain in his expression.

His soft, agonised, 'Oh, my God,' made her close her eyes and keep them closed, just long enough for him to cross the space that divided them.

Courage tensed automatically as she felt him take hold of her.

'It hurt so much to hear you say something like that when I'd wanted...waited...' Courage told him shakily from the protection of his arms.

'I was a fool—a jealous, love-crazed fool,' Gideon acknowledged.

'It hurt even more later... After... afterwards, when you held me as though... When you pretended to be so tender, so caring...so loving.'

'I wasn't pretending. That was exactly how I did feel, and, my God, how I hated myself for being so weak, and you as well, for witnessing my weakness. Can we start again, Courage, or is it too late?' he begged as he looked down at her.

'I...'

'We could start again right from the beginning,' Gideon promised throatily, whispering the words in her ear as he drew her closer. 'Right from the very beginning... that very first night when I reached out in the darkness and found I was holding a dream... my love in my arms.

'You kissed me so sweetly that night... Can you remember...? I touched your lips, your mouth, and you trembled so hard I was afraid that you might actually faint.'

'I was shocked... afraid... I'd never felt like that—never guessed I could feel like that... It was all so new to me...'

'And to me,' Gideon told her huskily. 'Just give me a chance, Courage. I'll court you properly, slowly... Let you take your time... set your own pace.'

'I'm afraid, Gideon,' Courage told him. 'Afraid of how much I want you... Afraid of loving you... Afraid of being hurt...'

But she still raised her face for his kiss, and clung tight to him as he wrapped his arms around her, kissing her with slow, deliberate sweetness while his heart hammered frantically against her body.

It was that that finally swept away her doubts; the knowledge that he was trying, for her sake, to exercise control, that emotionally he was as vulnerable and apprehensive as she was herself. She could see it in his eyes as they looked down into her own, feel it in the fine tremor of his hands as he held her, the unsteady thud of his heart.

'I want to go home with you,' she told him shyly. 'To... I want to be with you...'

'If I take you back with me now there's no way I'll be able to stop myself from wanting you to share my bed,' Gideon warned her.

'Perhaps that's what we should do,' Courage told him gravely. 'Wipe out the bad memories with new ones.'

'What are you reading?' Courage asked Gideon sleepily, as she burrowed closer to the warmth of his body, her mouth curling in a feminine smile of pleasure as she recalled their lovemaking earlier in the evening. She had no doubts now that Gideon loved her. Even if he hadn't told her so, repeating his words over and over again, she would have known it just from the way he touched her...

'This,' Gideon told her, showing her the sheets of paper covered in her own familiar writing. 'I picked it up at your grandmother's.'

'That's private,' Courage protested, but she was too happy to feel any real resentment.

'I don't deserve this...you...' Gideon told her heavily. 'Not after the way I treated you, the way I hurt you...'

'It's over,' Courage reminded him gently. 'It's over...'

'No, it isn't,' Gideon corrected her. 'This is just the beginning. Is your grandmother well enough to spend a few hours away from the recuperative centre, do you think?'

'Yes, I should imagine so,' Courage confirmed, frowning slightly. 'Why?'

'I thought you'd want her to be there when we get married ... And there's no way I'm waiting until she's discharged. You will marry me, won't you, Courage?' he asked her, suddenly heartachingly unsure of himself.

In answer Courage sat up in bed beside him, wrapping her arms around him, her breasts pressed against the warmth of his chest as she kissed him teasingly on the mouth, punctuating her kisses with laughter. 'Yes.'

He had hurt her badly—cruelly. But, loving him as much as she did, she could well understand how his own emotions had driven him to such extremes, and more importantly she knew that he was not by nature either vindictive or cruel, and that she need have no fear that such behaviour would ever recur.

'Do you think you'll ever really be able to forgive me?' he asked her quietly now, almost as though he had read her mind.

'I might,' Courage responded, the look in her eyes belying the laughter in her voice. 'Especially if you kiss me...

'Gideon ... Gideon ... what are you doing?' she protested huskily, as he reached out and snapped off the bedside light and then lowered her back against the bed.

'Kissing you—what else?' came his muffled response as he cupped her face and covered her mouth with his own. 'Isn't that what you wanted ...?'

'Mmm ... Mmm ...' was Courage's only response.

UNLOCK THE DOOR TO GREAT ROMANCE
AT BRIDE'S BAY RESORT

Join Harlequin's new across-the-lines series, set in an exclusive hotel on an island off the coast of South Carolina.

Seven of your favorite authors will bring you exciting stories about fascinating heroes and heroines discovering love at Bride's Bay Resort.

Look for these fabulous stories coming to a store near you beginning in January 1996.

Harlequin American Romance #613 in January
Matchmaking Baby by Cathy Gillen Thacker

Harlequin Presents #1794 in February
Indiscretions by Robyn Donald

Harlequin Intrigue #362 in March
Love and Lies by Dawn Stewardson

Harlequin Romance #3404 in April
Make Believe Engagement by Day Leclaire

Harlequin Temptation #588 in May
Stranger in the Night by Roseanne Williams

Harlequin Superromance #695 in June
Married to a Stranger by Connie Bennett

Harlequin Historicals #324 in July
Dulcie's Gift by Ruth Langan

Visit Bride's Bay Resort each month wherever Harlequin books are sold.

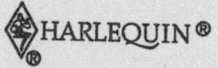

HARLEQUIN  PRESENTS®

It's the wedding of the month!

The latest in our tantalizing new selection of stories...

Wedlocked!

Bonded in matrimony, torn by desire...

Coming next month:

THE BRIDE IN BLUE
by Miranda Lee
Harlequin Presents #1811

The author whom everyone's talking about!

It was Sophia's wedding day, but she wasn't a happy and radiant bride. How could she be when she wasn't marrying Godfrey, the father of the baby she was expecting...but his younger brother instead? Jonathon Parnell was ruthlessly carrying out the deathbed promise he's made to Godfrey: to marry Sophia and look after their child. Jonathon claimed he wanted Sophia only as a wife of convenience, but Sophia suspected that, actually, Jonathon wanted *her*...

Available in May wherever Harlequin books are sold.

HARLEQUIN  PRESENTS®

—where satisfaction is guaranteed!

Coming next month, two classic stories
by your favorite authors:

FORGOTTEN HUSBAND
by Helen Bianchin
Harlequin Presents #1809

They said he was her husband...

But Elise didn't feel married to Alejandro Santanas, or
the mother of his unborn child. The accident had destroyed
her memory of the past few months. Had she really been in
love with this handsome stranger—and would he expect
that passion again?

ONE NIGHT OF LOVE
by Sally Wentworth
Harlequin Presents #1810

Once bitten, twice shy!

Oliver Balfour was the most attractive man Dyan had ever
met. But she wasn't going to mix business with pleasure.
From experience Dyan knew that a man like Oliver
would stalk a woman like her by lying his way into her
affections...and then go quickly for the kill in her bed!

Harlequin Presents—the best has just gotten better!
Available in May wherever Harlequin books are sold.

**Where there's a will there's a way...
for four charismatic characters to find true love**

by Sandra Marton

When Charles Landon dies, he leaves behind a different
legacy for each of his children.

As Cade, Grant, Zach and Kyra react to the terms of
their father's will, each receives an unexpected yet
delightful bequest: a very special love affair
that will last a lifetime.

Coming next month

**Book 2: *Guardian Groom*
Harlequin Presents #1813**

Grant has been left with the responsibility of acting
as Crista Adams's guardian, and he—who has never
let a woman get under his skin—suddenly finds
himself extremely jealous of every other man in
Crista's life. So Grant decides that Crista must
move in with him—and finds that he keeps *both* eyes
firmly fixed on her! Will life ever be the same again?

**Harlequin Presents—you'll want to know what
happens next!**

Available in May wherever Harlequin books are sold.

Fall in love all over again with

This Time... MARRIAGE

In this collection of original short stories, three brides get a unique chance for a return engagement!

- Being kidnapped from your bridal shower by a one-time love can really put a crimp in your wedding plans! *The Borrowed Bride*— by **Susan Wiggs**, *Romantic Times* Career Achievement Award-winning author.

- After fifteen years a couple reunites for the sake of their child—this time will it end in marriage? *The Forgotten Bride*—by **Janice Kaiser.**

- It's tough to make a good divorce stick—especially when you're thrown together with your ex in a magazine wedding shoot! *The Bygone Bride*— by **Muriel Jensen.**

Don't miss THIS TIME...MARRIAGE, available in April wherever Harlequin books are sold.

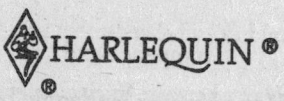 **HARLEQUIN** ®

HARLEQUIN PRESENTS®

Ever felt the excitement of forbidden passion?
Ever been thrilled by feverish desire?

Then you'll enjoy our selection of
dangerously sensual stories.

Take a chance on

Dangerous Liaisons

Falling in love is a risky affair!

Coming next month:

THAT MAN CALLAHAN!
by Catherine Spencer
Harlequin Presents #1812

Mike Callahan is sexy, handsome, magnetic—and out to win at
all costs! Isobel Whitelaw is cool, calm, professional—and
determined to keep Mike Callahan at arm's length!

From the moment he marched into her office, she knew he was
trouble! And soon he had invaded every corner of her life. But
Isobel had been burned before and had made herself immune
to love and desire.

So why couldn't Isobel resist that man Callahan?

Available in May wherever Harlequin books are sold.